A Singer of Thrace

K-Nurse Book Three

By Mark Leo Tapper

Sousa House Press

Barre, Vermont 05641

ASIN: B09P1Z9WD5

Cover design by Marianne Nowicki

For John and Michele

And when all at once the god stopped
her, and with pain in his voice
spoke the words: he has turned around–,
she couldn't grasp this and quietly said: who?

Orpheus, Eurydice, Hermes
Rainer Maria Rilke

The Furies who avenge men's sin,
Who at the guilty's terror grin,
Let tears of sorrow from them steal;
No longer does the turning wheel
Ixion's head send whirling round;
Old Tantalus upon the sound
Forgets the waters and his thirst,
And while the music is rehearsed
The vulture ceases flesh to shred.
At last the monarch of the dead
In tearful voice, "We yield," he said

Boethius, *The Consolation of Philosophy*, 523 A.D

PART ONE

One

My forehead throbbed over my right eye. I tried to rub it, but I couldn't move my hand because it was bound. As were my feet. And I was upside down. The good news, to the extent there was any, was that sunshine in the Ether is always weak, even on a sunny day, so at least the light didn't hurt my eyes when I opened them. That was it for the good news.

My hands and feet were tied together around a stout pole, which was carried on the shoulders of two cogs who looked straight ahead, walking in matched cadence. Craning my neck to get a look at my surroundings made my head throb more fiercely, so I closed my eyes again and focused on my breathing.

I may have slept, or just passed out, but when I woke the cogs were exchanging a traditional greeting, and both voices came from above my head, so a new player had entered the game.

"On the same page," said Cog One.

"Moving forward," replied Cog Two.

"The involuntary guest appears to have suboptimal wellness."

"I won't crystal ball his outcomes, but his suboptimal wellness will permit the facilitators to extract, unpack, and operationalize the guest's information."

"At a minimum we can level-set for the next vermin who appears."

"Yes, the bosses are obsessed with level-setting this group to establish a baseline."

Vermin, in case you were wondering, are the Knight-Nurses of the Order of St. John. The cogs have *one* colorful noun, and it's to describe us as loathsome pests.

I find that very hurtful.

While having my own submerged metaphor ––even if it was an unflattering one-- made me feel special, that feeling was wrestled to the ground and choked out by the knowledge that I was about to have a really bad day.

I can't die in the Ether, none of the K-Nurses can, but, as evidenced by the pulsing in my forehead, we can suffer. On those rare occasions when one of us was captured between our real world death and rebirth, the Returned had a whole theme park of pain waiting for us. I had died defending Fort St. Elmo in 1565. I would have to endure whatever they did to me until I was called back to the world and reborn.

When reborn, I would get a childhood mercifully free of slashing, hacking, crushing, etc. And then, sometime in my early twenties, the bastards back at headquarters would awaken me, and in awakening, I would remember whatever they were about to do to me today.

My last memory before being bonked on the head in the Ether was fighting the Ottoman hordes beside Jude. We were hacking away at soldiers who leapt over piles of their own dead, holding our own on the remnants of Fort St Elmo on Malta. Eventually though, Jude was cut down next to me, and a Turkish knight thrust his lance into my head at a full gallop.

No wonder my head hurt so much.

The cogs were careful to ram me into the metal doors of the Central City Strategic Wellness Ecosystem on the way in. Their torture chamber occupied the hospital (Strategic Wellness Ecosystem) basement, an irony not lost on any of us who had been involuntary guests.

"On the same page," said the cog, dragging me by my right arm.

"Moving forward," replied the sentry, who ticked something on his clipboard and nodded to take me downstairs.

It's always downstairs. Why can't you have a dungeon, a torture chamber, or even just a prison cell upstairs? Sure, you don't want big windows or a lot of natural light. I get that; you're trying to create a mood, an ambiance. But it doesn't always have to be below grade. As I have said before, the Returned are hampered by a lack of imagination.

"Hey," I said, chin pointing at the sentry, "Are you guys related? Something about the eyes. Cousins, maybe?"

The cogs regarded me without a change in expression. They all look alike, I mean *exactly* alike, the same patch of short, coarse, black hair on their heads, the same expressionless face, milky complexion, gray eyes, and prominent foreheads with bushy black eyebrows.

"Maybe somebody's daddy was popular in the village? If you know what I mean." I tried to elbow the cog to my right in conspiratorial friendship and missed completely. "A scoundrel, that's what I'm trying to say. Maybe your dad was a scoundrel. I'm not judging, don't get me wrong, but," before I could finish, the sentry filled my mouth with a coarse cloth and secured it around the back of my head. Then I remembered that all cogs were men, no females at all. They were made in a flask or something. The joke was on me.

"The meaning aspect of Vermin speech is entirely beyond me," said the sentry.

"The bosses understand," the other cog replied. "They're going to do a deep dive on this one."

"High-level drill-down for sure."

Even if I was fluent in cogspeak, which I am not, that didn't sound good. It sounds *suboptimal*, I thought, with the same pride I had when I had learned to count to ten in Spanish.

Two hours later, the stump of my left wrist was still spouting blood after my discussion with the first inquisitor. I had the last laugh, though, because to nail me to the wall they had to use a spike through my elbow. Couldn't use my hand. Suboptimal crucifixion.

The crucifixion wall occupied the lower half of one side of the square room, whose ceiling disappeared among wires, pipes, and beams that looked made of metal. Somewhere above, a pipe dripped making a muffled clanging sound as regular as the swish of a horse's tail chasing away flies. Half-way up the wall, the room was circled by a catwalk that also appeared to be made of metal. A stairway descended from it to the torture area proper.

"Paul, dear Paul, sweet, sweet Paul," purred a deep female voice from the walkway above me. "How have you been, buddy?"

If the concept of sexual arousal, in all of its forms and manifestations, could be molded into a being, it would have been Lilith, senior vice president and chief operating officer of The Company. She was Thaumiel's number two. One of Lilith's magics was that she could shift her form to be pleasing to whomever she was manipulating. For me, she was curvy, like one of the rich women the Hospitaller muckety-mucks were always entertaining. Her hair fell in curls over her shoulders. The gown she wore, a shiny silver, showed cleavage without being bawdy.

"My lady graces a poor knight?" I replied, spitting blood and at least one tooth. "The paint on your face is remarkable. The snake's tongue is a little off-putting, but those hooves are marvelous."

She looked at her feet, clad in reddish brown slippers and chuckled.

"Good to see you haven't lost your sense of humor," she said, walking down the stairs to the pit where I was impaled. Her shoes clicked on each step. "I hope your memory is as good as ever."

My left eye was like a boiled egg in my head, useless and squishy, but I could still see pretty well out of my right one.

"What kind of leather are those shoes, anyway?" I asked. As long as I kept her talking, no one was cutting any part of me off. I just had to stall long enough to disappear. Time works differently in the Ether, so I could pop away any minute, or I could be here for weeks. Lilith would be sure it felt like weeks either way.

"These old things?" she said, flicking her long, dark hair over her shoulder. "I think these are baby skin." She turned to the cog standing at the doorway, who nodded. "Not cog baby skin, either. The rift is growing big enough for us to bring souvenirs back with us when we are expelled."

I strained against the spikes holding me in place and roared. I screamed a death incantation as she disemboweled me with one long nail, but my magic was only a trickle here.

I vomited blood, and the next thing I remember, I was a toddler hiding under a cow to escape a beating from my mother for laughing in church.

Two

The yacht rocked softly under me in the calm sea. On the highest deck, Augustine, hiding from the sun in a hoodie and covered down to her closed-toe shoes, was engrossed in a leather-bound book with a lock on its covers. The book was so big I could see it from the railing, so it was likely some kind of grimoire or guide to arcanum, Augustine's idea of beach reading. Simon slept beside me, his chair tipped back, straw hat shading his face, his tan glowed in the late afternoon sun. With his feet on the railing, I expected him to crash backward at any minute, but his balance did not falter, even in his sleep.

My bandaged arms rested on the same railing. I was recovering from third degrees burns while sitting right beside our sleeping fire mage. The three months since we fled our destroyed headquarters had brought little healing to my arms or to my spirit. The sun glowed happily above, splashing light on the sparkling water. Somewhere bands were playing, and somewhere children shout, I thought. My mood was as black as the char on my forearms.

I had burned them trying to follow my daughter, Aurora, through a metal door into a maelstrom of fire. Unable to open it with magic, I assaulted the door with my arms and hands, which were burned to a crisp in the process. And I had failed to save

Aurora. My daughter, my greatest joy in nine hundred years, was gone, prisoner in a realm we knights only visited in the time between mortal death and our rebirths.

Because she had not entered the Ether by dying, we had no idea how to get her back to our world. Aurora was there, and she was still alive, and I couldn't bear the thought of it, so I would do anything to bring her back.

"That sunshine is going to be real good for your burns," Phil said, pulling up a chair.

"Can't even feel it."

"Of course you can't feel it. Those are third-degree burns. The nerves are damaged. You know this," Phil squinted out toward the horizon. "Don't be a git," he said.

"Don't be a twat," I replied.

"You're both cunts," Simon said, without opening his eyes.

A feminine voice made a tsking sound, and the scent of lilac drifted by.

"Morning, Barbara," we said in unison. Barbara was the best seer I had ever known. She could open windows into the Ether at will. Her house was back in South Carolina, a couple of miles from our ruined headquarters. She had an on-again-off-again relationship with Augustine, and she was too openly associated with our order to leave her behind.

"Good morning, boys. And I use the term advisedly. Why are you such pigs? And so early in the day?"

"Oink," replied Simon.

I chuckled, but seeing Barbara's expression, forced a frown.

"Sorry," Phil murmured.

Barbara sighed before she, too, pulled up a seat.

"Paul, Thomas wants to have a look at your arms," Barbara began. "They are healing too slowly, and he thinks he should intervene."

Thomas, our most powerful spell slinger (he knocked me on my ass the last time I called him that), wanted to magic my burns away. I had my reasons for holding off.

"Not until we have a plan," I said, trying for a monotone.

"There's no reason you should suffer until then."

"There's lots of reasons. We don't want to use a drop of magic that we don't have to. With Roosevelt in the White House and fascism on the rise everywhere, we've got to conserve every little bit."

"He's not wrong," Phil interjected. "We've got our hands full. If we're going to mount a rescue operation on top of all that, we're going to have to be careful. We can't wait twenty years for the Council to be at full strength again. We need Aurora."

Barbara pulled her lips into a pout.

"I suppose," she said.

"Gotta spend magic to make magic," Simon groused.

We ignored him.

Peter appeared on the mezzanine that jutted out from the second floor. He hooked his head toward the interior, and we all got up to join him. Above, Augustine closed her book, and shaking her head at us, disappeared down a ladder to the second floor.

Our benefactor, the yacht's owner, had provided for all of our needs. The boat's capacious storage below decks housed those weapons that we had been able to retrieve from the ruins of our headquarters. Each knight had their own cabin. A helicopter was chained to the front deck, its wings folded and covered. The ship even came with a chef and steward, who were setting out a buffet in the sitting area we had made into our council chambers.

I filled my plate with about twenty little stuffed croissants. The food was amazing, but the portions were less than what I had become accustomed to in the United States. We sat in the same order we had arranged ourselves in for centuries. Peter was at the head of what would have been a table if we had had a table, and the chair facing him, Aurora's place, was left empty. Simon was last to sit down, because he was stuck at the blender making a drink that would have been garnished with little umbrellas at a restaurant.

We said our oath: "To comfort the sick and to oppose evil, our lives are not our own."

With Aurora gone, it felt empty and sad, like eating a rice cake.

"Updates on the situation in the US," Peter said, turning to Andrew.

"Not good," he began, "not good at all. Roosevelt has closed the borders; no one in or out. There have been some arrests, mostly those openly opposing the administration. For now, they are held in ICE detention camps, but we have information that the Department of Homeland Security is building 're-education' facilities in each administrative region of the country. Private contractors have also been hired to expand federal prisons in each territory."

"Paul keeps telling us the Returned lack any creativity," Augustine said. "And while it hurts me to agree with him," she shot me a half-smile, "They do seem to be following *Despotism By The Numbers*."

"We have seen this many times before," Peter agreed. "I am shocked that this particular pattern repeats itself over and over and yet, it is a surprise to so many."

"The last time this played out, Phil and I were dead in the first week of the war," Bart said.

"So this is our personal best?" Phil asked.

"No war yet," I reminded them.

"That's only a matter of time," said Andrew, tamping down his annoyance at being interrupted. He's the counselor to the council, a psychiatric nurse with emotional control not of this earth. "Augustine, Peter, Bart, and Phil will contact any remaining human assets we have and see if we can establish a resistance before Roosevelt gets to full police state."

"Resistance? Like in France?" James asked, looking up from his laptop.

"Just like France in the last big war," Andrew agreed.

"I'd like to be a part of that," James said.

"I was hoping you and I could spearhead the propaganda effort," said Andrew. "That leaves Thomas, Simon, and Paul."

"To bring Aurora back," I said, looking into his eyes.

"To bring Aurora back," he replied, without breaking the gaze.

Three

The new portal Barbara opened looked exactly like the last eleven: a bleak, sandy, treeless plain with jagged mountains in the background.

"Are you sure you're not just looking through the same window over and over?" Simon asked, his face showing instant regret at the question.

Barbara glared at him, twisted her hand in the air, and the scene disappeared. She inhaled sharply, hands on hips, and exhaled with her eyes closed.

Simon gulped.

He was a powerful sorcerer, a fire master, but he was afraid of Barbara's temper.

Hell, we were all afraid of Barbara's temper.

"Darling," said Barbara, turning to me, "would you tell the Heat Miser to settle down?"

"Barbara says shut it," I murmured in Simon's direction.

He nodded.

"Let's talk about what's going on here," Barbara said.

"Look, I'm sorry," Simon whined.

"I'm not talking about you, idiot," she huffed, "I mean what's going on in the Ether. Usually, I can find one of you there, because your energy is so different, so unusual, that it sticks out. It calls to me."

"That's how you were able to find Jude," said Thomas.

"Precisely," Barbara replied. "When one of you is in the Ether, I can feel it. I haven't had that much practice, only three of you have been through rebirth in my lifetime, but the call, the pull of you there is unmistakable. When you all went to the Ether for Aurora's ceremony, I was practically hallucinating."

"So why can't you locate Aurora?" Thomas asked.

"I honestly don't know," she replied.

"I think I do," I said. "When Jude appeared to us before the attack, he told me that Aurora was a cuckoo, those birds who hide their eggs in another bird's nest. She was the hatchling he had hidden with us. He said the Ether was her home."

"So she is one of them?" Thomas asked, his face now a mask.

"He might just have been taunting me, twisting the knife," I said.

"But that might explain why Barbara can't find her."

"It might," I conceded.

"I never felt any Returned on her," Thomas said. "I don't believe it."

"I don't believe it either," Simon added. "But what if we assume it's true, game it out. If she is somehow connected with the Returned, connected with the Ether, we aren't going to be able to find her through Barbara. Someone will have to go there, find her, and bring her home."

"That person would be dead and reborn by the end of the first week," Thomas huffed. "The power required to maintain a physical presence in the Ether would whittle you away to nothing in days. You'd die, enter the Ether in your original form, then be reborn, and we'd be down another mage for the coming battles. Our community has already made too many sacrifices to waste another knight."

Thomas still felt guilty for the body he occupied. He had not been reborn, but had possessed a willing supporter, Miguel, who would die when Thomas died and who was all but dead now, just a sleeping consciousness. We had taken the shortcut, not waiting for Thomas to be reborn and grow, because the rising tide that was supporting the Returned's CEO, Garridan Roosevelt, would need all of our power to turn back.

"You'd need to be camouflaged somehow, to look like one of the cogs," I said. "And warded, so they couldn't sense you."

"That's a lot of juice," said Simon. "Even Thomas wouldn't last more than two or three days using that much magic."

Thomas paced, deep in thought, and we were quiet.

"We could Captain Planet the spell," Simon said under his breath.

"We could what now?" I asked.

"By our powers combined," Thomas replied. "A group spell similar to the one we used to banish Jude. It still wouldn't last more than two or three days, but we could distribute the magical burden among the whole council. The younger bodies could contribute more, balance things out."

"Thank heaven I have a disciplined skin care routine," Simon added. "Even with some wrinkles, I will still be looking good. The rest of you who don't even moisturize, I'm looking at you, Paul, well . . ." He tutted.

I made a show of ignoring him but found myself touching the skin on my cheek.

"That still doesn't solve the problem of how to get Aurora's body out of the Ether. If I'm camouflaged to the cogs, how do we know Barbara will be able to see me?"

"Who says *you're* going?" Thomas asked, rounding on me.

I squared off and set my feet.

"She's my daughter. I have to go."

"We all love Aurora, and I'm the obvious choice."

We stared at each other. I was pretty sure he blinked before I did, but I know he would deny it.

"For fuck's sake!" Barbara cried. "What is wrong with you? Does having a penis remove all reason?"

"I think it's the balls that remove reason," Simon offered, then winced at Barbara's expression.

"Stop this right now," Barbara said, her voice brooking no objection. "The Council will decide who goes and how to get Aurora back. This insane posturing isn't getting us one millimeter closer to the goal."

I have been trained to respond to that tone of voice in dozens of incarnations, we all have. This is the tone of the angry mother, and just like Pavlov's dog, we were conditioned, not to drool, but to put our tails between our legs. Mommy is angry. Be quiet and don't argue. This tone of voice never slows Augustine (or Perpetua, when she's around) at all. As far as I knew, Barbara never had any children, so I'm not sure how she had perfected the mother voice, probably from having to be around us.

"I'm sorry," I said, looking at Thomas.

He grunted, nodded, and turned away.

"We'll talk to the Council and figure it out," I said. "You're right. It would be stupid to plan this without the others."

"Of course I'm right," said Barbara, sniffing.

We three men slouched toward the door.

"Besides," Simon quipped, "we all know the Council is going to send me to rescue Aurora." He made a little flame dance from fingertip-to-fingertip.

I cuffed him on the back of the head, but he only chuckled.

Four

Peter brought the Council to order with a nod to Barbara, who sat outside of the council circle. Barbara was the most powerful of the seers, but she had no magic except the ability to open windows into the Ether. She could look around, but she couldn't enter, and she certainly couldn't stop anything that tried to come through from the other side.

Over the years she had gained a good sense of the terrain. The Ring, a range of mountains that encircled Central City on every side except the northwest. There the city had been built right up to the sea. Between the Ring and the City, the Wastes stretched sand dunes right up to the city gates.

Barbara was not our only seer, though. John "The Trucker" Drain, who lived on the west coast, could open windows into the Ether, too, but he couldn't sense knights, but he could do reconnaissance. He emailed us detailed drawings, and James was working on putting the digital images together to make as good a map as we could.

"We have considered your idea that perhaps Aurora was somehow made in the Ether or from the Ether," Peter began.

"It makes sense," Augustine finished. "But we don't have any idea what their end game is. Why did they want her raised by us? Has kidnapping her been part of their plan all along?"

"There are also inconsistencies," Peter continued, glancing at Augustine. "Our magic is greatly reduced in the Ether because we are not part of its inherent magic, it's natal energy. That must also be true for the Returned, who are originally from our world; they have great magic here but must have much less in the Ether. I don't understand how, if Aurora was truly from the Ether, she could have manifested such power in our world."

Peter's words gave me hope; maybe Aurora wasn't one of the Returned's monsters in disguise. If she could use so much magic here, in our world, some of her was from here. She wasn't entirely a creature of the Ether.

Peter said, "To bring her home we will need to send one of you to that terrible place."

"We have no way of knowing what kind of shape she will be in," interjected Andrew, our shrink. "They may be torturing her, and she already has some challenges, her eating disorder most importantly. Every day we delay worries me more about the woman who will return."

"She won't get much in the way of food," Simon muttered. "They have exactly two meals there: gruel and stew. That's enough to put anyone off their feed."

"If we can devise a way to send our knight there without being detected, he will be invisible to Barbara, which will make extraction more difficult," Peter added. "He will need,"

"Or she," Augustine said, glaring at Peter.

"Or she," he agreed. "Will need a way to signal us so that Barbara can open a portal. When the window has been opened, those knights remaining here on the boat will extract Aurora and her escort."

We all stared at Peter, whose gaze fell on each of us in turn.

"Knowing the danger and what's at stake, I will only take a volunteer to,"

Before he finished, we were all on our feet. Peter's face darkened.

"Perhaps just once in this meeting I will finish my thought," he said. There was nervous chuckling at that. Peter sighed. "I suppose since Paul is the one who brought Aurora to us, he must be the one to bring her back."

"Thank you, my lord," I croaked, tears streaming down my face. Philip gripped my shoulder. They all looked away to give me a moment to compose myself. I wiped my face and took a deep breath. When I looked up, Simon met my gaze.

"Your fly is down," he said.

I looked down to my pants and the room exploded into laughter. Augustine wrapped me in a hug.

"Idiot men," she said between snickers.

"We still haven't figured out how to get me in there," I said.

"I have run the calculations," Thomas began, "and the cost of sending your body there is just too high. Even if we pool our magic, two or three days in the Ether would take ten or more years from all of our lives."

"That's a price we can afford to pay," Andrew said.

"Not if we are to have any hope of prevailing against Thaumiel," Peter declared, and there was such finality in his tone that I had to remind myself that this was a council of equals.

The rumbling among council members rose.

"I think I have a workaround," Thomas said, holding up his hands. "Paul has explained this process to you before." Thomas gestured at his own body. Peter's head dropped, but he said nothing.

"We send Paul's mind to take over a cog?" Augustine asked.

"Exactly," Thomas replied. "If he possesses a cog, the Returned shouldn't be able to sense him there. If we pick the right cog, Paul will be able to move around more-or-less freely to find Aurora."

"Hold up," Simon interjected. "That will only work if the cog agrees to the possession. Why would a cog ever do that?"

"Marketing, advertising, these beings are suckers for it. It shouldn't be too hard to convince them they are getting some kind of deal. Andrew can come up with the campaign," said Thomas.

"But when I return the cog will die," I said under my breath.

Peter heard me, his head snapping up.

"A casualty of war," he said.

I sighed.

"Will I be able to stay there indefinitely?"

"Three days," Thomas replied. "For about a year of life from all of us, we can send you for three days. Your body will stay here, where I can watch over it. We'll bring your consciousness and Aurora back through Barbara's windows."

"How am I supposed to find them?" Barbara snapped. "I won't be able to get a lock on their location."

Thomas produced something from his pocket, and we all leaned forward.

"What the hell?" Bart asked.

"That's a pit from one of the dates we had for breakfast," Augustine said. "So?"

"The pit is too small for Barbara to feel," Thomas explained. "Paul will have to plant it when he gets there. It will grow enough in three days that Barbara will be able to find it."

"Genetically engineered?" asked James.

"Enchanted," Thomas replied. "Should be a full-grown tree in three days."

"Why dates, though?" asked Phil.

Thomas gave Phil a moment to work it out.

"Because the Ether is mostly desert," Phil said, answering his own question.

Peter nodded once to himself.

"Paul," he said, "prepare yourself. You leave tonight."

Five

Since I wasn't traveling in the flesh, I didn't have anything to pack. Preparing mentally for the journey was another matter entirely. In order to possess another body, I needed to lock out my other preoccupations. The gut-wrenching fear for Aurora and the terrible guilt at taking a life were the biggest distractions. I had killed many times in battle and some times out of necessity, but not an innocent. This cog, whoever he was, hadn't hurt anyone, hadn't threatened anyone. He was just a guy going about his life. I tried to rationalize, but the guilt wouldn't go away.

I was also guilty of thinking that a cog life was worth less than a human one. That kind of belief played right into the hands of the Returned: devaluing and de-humanizing the "other." Biologically, cogs were almost human with some significant differences. They were decanted, not born, cloned from one "uber" cog. Because of that, and because there was no need for, or tolerance of, diversity in their culture, they were all male. That fact alone made me scream with fury and terror; my daughter was in a place where the only other woman, Lilith, had taken the mantel Queen of the Night. In order to pass safely into a cog's body, I had to clear all this from my mind and heart.

And I had to learn to speak cog. The basic structure of cogspeak is similar to English. It uses many of the same words, but with different meanings, think unadulterated corporate speak, and you've got the main idea. They would use common words in twisted ways to inflate or disguise their meaning. Cogs also spoke with little inflection, no changes in volume or emphasis, no changes in facial expressions.

Barbara was the expert on cogspeak, since she had spent more time listening to it than any member of the Council. Whenever we arrived in the Ether after our human death, we spent all the time trying to avoid the cogs, so we rarely got to hear them speaking to each other.

"I need you to ingest the deliverables at the SWE," Barbara said.

I stuttered for a moment, my mind racing.

"Make your face still, or you won't last ten minutes," she said.

I closed my eyes and relaxed my shoulders, then my face.

"Is this a delivery?" I asked, tentatively.

"Very good. Where is the delivery?"

"The SWE."

"Which stands for what?"

"Special Weekend Enterprise?"

Barbara huffed.

"Space for Wandering Efficiencies?"

"You are going to die and Aurora will be lost to us forever."

My eyes narrowed.

"Still your face!" Barbara commanded. "SWE is Strategic Wellness Ecosystem. It's like a hospital."

I went very still, the memory of Lilith disemboweling me was vivid and alarming and seemed to be happening right there on the yacht. Flashbacks suck hard.

"I know that place," I said, my voice cracking.

"They use acronyms as often as they can, even when it's completely unnecessary. 'SL' is shoelace, for example. As in the phrase, 'your SL is un-normalized.'"

"That should be easy to remember," I said. I pulled my lips out of a pout before she could yell at me again.

"Sports analogies are good, too. 'Moving the ball down field' and 'going downtown,' you hear these kinds of things a lot."

"What in the name of St. Cuthbert is 'going downtown.'"

"I don't know," Barbara admitted. "Something from basketball, I think."

"They have basketball in the Ether?"

"There aren't any sports that I could see. They just use the idioms the Returned bring back to them. Remember that cogspeak originated in the Ether. It came into our world with the Returned. They have been so successful at infiltrating our economic leadership, that now we use a lot of it. When they get sent back to the Ether, the Returned bring back expressions from our world."

"A meaningful exchange of idioms," I harped, knowing that my face betrayed my disgust.

"Cogs have zero interest in where the expressions come from, pretty much zero curiosity period," Barbara explained.

"This is impossible," I said, and even I heard the whining in my voice. Then I had a vision of Aurora, nailed to the basement wall in the SWE, Lilith and her minions carving pieces off her. Aurora's real body was present in the Ether. She would return with all the damage they did to her.

"Forget I said that." I relaxed my face, feeling the expression draining away. "Hit me."

"Your attire has suboptimal interoperability."

"Your clothes don't match," I said, careful not to smile.

Barbara nodded.

"Although," Barbara mused, "they have no real color there, so I can't imagine how that could be."

"I'm going to meet you where you are and say that your abstraction playbook is not fully operationalized."

Barbara's jaw hung open.

"And try not to normalize that facial aspect. It is too emotion adjacent. You should level-set bidirectional resting face with me."

Barbara bowed low in front of her chair.

"I am crystal-balling full enterprise efficiencies," Barbara said, her face utterly neutral, "and anticipating extraction outcomes that are a compass point for locking in a success driver."

Now I bowed low.

"Master," I said, keeping my face as still as a death mask.

Barbara smiled in a way that might have been flirting if she wasn't an oracle and I wasn't nine hundred years old. Besides, Barbara and Augustine had been together a long time, and while I

30

was sure Augustine would be open-minded, I really didn't need any more drama before my departure.

"What have you been able to gather on the cog I'm going to possess?" I asked.

"We don't need a lot of details, after all. He's a cog. Andrew can predict his behavior with a high degree of accuracy. What makes this cog different is that he is a servant in the Corner Office Building, where the Returned live. He can move around more freely than most of the others. You're going to need that if you have any hope of finding Aurora in the three days you'll be over there."

"Andrew isn't going, I am. But I take your point; don't get creative. With all that uniformity, how am I going to get Aurora anywhere? Assuming I can find her, and I can free her, she's going to stick out. And even if I plant the date pit just outside the city, we'll at least have to get that far."

"That's why they pay you the big bucks."

"That's why I get the big bucks," I repeated, and, groaning, I shuffled to my room for some sleep before the ritual at moonrise.

Six

The last purple light of dusk was disappearing behind the horizon as I took off my shirt and prepared for the ghastly insertion of tubes. In the movies, when a body is being kept in stasis, it's frozen or something, no poop or pee, no water or food. The movie-going public doesn't even question it. A body gotta do what a body gotta do, even if the mind running it has left the building.

Luckily, I was surrounded by nurses. The IV for fluids was inserted in the crook of my left elbow, while I positioned myself on the cholera cot. One of the defining symptoms of cholera is "rice-water stools." In really bad cases you essentially shit yourself to death. The cots were developed to allow diarrhea to flow into a bucket so that patients too weak to get to a latrine wouldn't constantly be soaked in their own feces. It was a pretty low-tech solution, a canvas cot with a big round hole for my butt to hang through and a bucket underneath.

There was also going to be a urinary catheter, but that would be inserted after my mind was in the ether. Having a long rubber hose snaked up your penis is not the worse thing ever, but, you know, it ain't fun.

Unfortunately the feeding tube would have to be inserted while I was still awake. A tube would be pushed through one nostril, down the back of my throat and into my stomach. I had to be awake to tell them if it went into my lung by mistake. Augustine inserted the tube while I madly sipped water from a straw to swallow it. This was not as bad as a catheter, but still not much fun. Augustine injected some air into the tube while listening for bubbling in my stomach to make sure the tube was in the right place. She taped it to my nose and nodded to herself.

With my orifices accounted for, I laid back on the cot. The other knights circled around me. Peter kissed my forehead and whispered a blessing.

"Bring her back," Augustine said. "I don't want to have to go after the two of you."

I winked at her and closed my eyes as the chanting began.

My mind's eye blurred into a maelstrom of black and gray spinning images, which resolved to an empty silver space where I hovered opposite a cog. His expressionless face reminded me how hard the impersonation was going to be.

"Are you A-6156?" I asked.

The cog nodded.

"What did they promise you for allowing me to use your body?"

"A day off," the cog replied, his mouth forming the words as if he was not sure how to pronounce them.

"Just one?"

"You can have more than one?" the cog asked. Then he made a grunting sound that I realized was what passed for laughter in the

Ether. "My sense of the time-off piece is not so understanding adjacent."

I sighed and walked toward him.

"Do you have it?" I asked extending my hand, palm open, the date pit surreal in the center of my outstretched hand. A physical object in the spirit realm was quite a trick. I doubt any of us but Thomas could have managed it. The cog held out his hand. In it was a gray rock. He had taken it from the Ether, and now its physical form, it's approximate size and mass would be replaced by the fig pit.

"Sweet dreams," I said as I touched him, and he faded.

"*Manus manum lavat.*"

That was the last thing I heard him say. A cog pronouncing Latin was like hearing a dog sing the Star Spangled Banner; even if you recognized every word, you are so awestruck that it goes right by you.

My eyes opened on a gray room, dimly lit. A window on one wall looked out onto the cement block of neighboring barracks not six feet away. Barbara had showed me cog sleeping rooms with rows of double-decker cots, so this room was apparently the height of cog luxury; it had only one bed.

The face in mirror wore heavy black brows, a bulbous nose, long ears with pendulous lobes, and a chin devoid of hair. As I saw no shaving implements, I had supposed that cogs did not have facial hair. The black stubble on my head, though, was sharp and stiff, like a horse brush, and my gray eyes stared back at me, vacuous.

I tried to smile but couldn't move my mouth that way. Neither could I frown. My worry about remaining expressionless had been for nothing. This face had limited movement. I couldn't even grimace. I was one of "the faceless hordes," and now that *expression* took on a whole new meaning.

The room was furnished in early apocalypse with distinctive Soviet influences, all right angles, utterly without decoration. The bed looked serviceable. The one table and chair was as practical as an umbrella in Seattle. The worn black area rug gave the room a homeyness that set me right at ease.

I tell a lie. The rug looked like a black beast had been shorn of its hair and the clippings glued together. This rug is where bad mustaches went to die. I despaired of ever crossing the room without unconsciously playing The Floor Is Lava. Edging around the hideous rug, I opened the only door and peered into the hallway.

Up and down the hall, at even intervals, stood doors exactly like mine, black metal frames surrounding ash-colored doors, no decorations, nothing to make any door different from its fellows in any way. The off-white hall stretched into a distant corner, where, no doubt, there was another row of doors.

How the hell was I going to find my way around? Any marking or insignia on the door or wall would stand out like a PETA member at a pig roast. Looking back into the room, I searched for anything that might help to identify this place from all the others, anything different. Of course, that was the point of this "culture;'" there was never anything different.

I wouldn't be doing much sleeping anyway. I closed the door watching it immediately disappear into the line of its fellows and knew I would never find it again. With the clock ticking, all my energy should be focused on finding Aurora; I only had three days, and I had no idea where to look.

Taking a fortifying breath, I turned and fell face-first into the hallway. First new information about cogs: they cannot stride or run. They move in short, steady steps. As I got more accustomed to this body, I learned to take the steps more rapidly, but for now, I was limited to a leisurely shuffle.

Off to find my little girl in an alien world, where I knew no one, had no idea where she had been taken, and had no magic to free her if I did find her.

For Aurora, I would have done it with all those limitations *blindfolded*. I wouldn't succeed, but I would do it anyway.

Seven

I shambled to an elevator marked EXIT, careful not to hurry while I was getting used to this new way of moving. The elevator opened onto a field of Astroturf bordered by a bicycle rack in which twenty or thirty identical bicycles stood like soldiers on parade. When they said EXIT, they really meant it.

I bent slowly to touch the plastic grass, which was stiff and springy, and, I imagined, would hurt to fall on. The craziest thing about it, though—even crazier than the acres and acres of the stuff—was that it was transparent, not green. In the dim light of the planet's three small moons, it looked like shallow water.

I skirted the edge of the field, heading for what looked like a road, when another cog appeared from a narrow alley between buildings.

"On the same page," he called without looking at me.

"Moving forward," I replied and raised my hand to wave.

He stopped.

"Is your upper extremity in need of wellness assistance, function-wise?"

I panicked, which, in this body, meant nothing at all. My heart rate didn't even rise.

"My upper extremity is level-setting its drivers of comfort."

"I hope you will fully operationalize it. Feel free to ping me for wellness opportunities," the cog answered, moving away.

"It is what it is," I said, trying to increase my speed without falling down again. "Positive feedback," I called after him.

On finding the road, I followed a line of cogs on bicycles heading toward a well-lit area. I rounded a non-descript corner and found myself in downtown Central City. Black-and-white signs, all in the same careful sans-serif print advertised: BEVERAGES and ENTERTAINMENT. There were stew houses and gruel joints that showed their wares on the signs over the doors. The bar signs said simply "BOOZE." None of the establishments had names that I could make out.

I was hungry and not feeling any need to be entertained –lord knows what cog entertainment would be--so I turned (carefully) into a stew house and sat down at an empty table. Before my butt had settled into the chair, a waiter arrived and set down a steaming bowl of something gray, and a spoon.

"Four credits," he said in a monotone.

I had forgotten to check for money. I reached into my pocket and was relieved to come out with a roll of bills. Relief couldn't register on my face, thankfully, and I was beginning to wonder if this body had any endocrine system at all. Peeling off a five credit note, I handed it to the waiter. He took the money, but otherwise stood still, looking at me. After an awkward moment, he inclined his head slightly and pushed his two eyebrows together so that it looked as if a woolly bear caterpillar was sleeping on his face.

He was obviously waiting for something. A tip? Did cogs tip? I had given him a fiver for a four dollar dish, so —then it hit me.

"Consider the balance an indication of positive feedback," I said.

"This is a net plus," he responded, returning to the kitchen.

The stew wasn't *bad*, exactly. It was mostly just textures. It didn't have any taste at all, just chunky, chewy bits and soft, squishy bits. The other diners ate their stew and talked, the monotone of their voices producing a uniform hum, all the same pitch and inflection. I tripped on my way out but was saved by grabbing the door frame. No one seemed to take notice.

A couple of doors down from the stew house was a beverage center (BOOZE). It was packed, every seat taken, and many cogs milled around saying heaven-knows-what as they collided with and bounced off each other.

A few were face down on the bar or on a table. That part was grim: colorless men, drinking to oblivion. The room did not reek like a comparable bar in our world, but the floor was sticky with whatever concoction was helping these unfortunates get numb. Maybe *number*. I kept ascribing feelings to them, which I thought then was a mistake, but later learned spoke unflattering volumes about me. A cog with a shirt like mine bumped my shoulder.

"Greetings A-6156. What is your wellness status?"

"Moving forward," I said, not knowing the right response.

"Your humor compass point is well curated," he said.

"It is what it is."

"Didn't we normalize your nocturnal work-shift?"

Oh shit. I was supposed to be at work.

"I may have locked in an excess of intoxicant," I admitted. "Could you blue sky the work playing field with me again."

His eyebrows rose.

"A-6156, surely this is an opportunity for growth. Better to ambulate your buttocks to the COB ASAP."

"I will expect negative feedback," I said, and tried to knit my brows. "Perhaps you could advance me the work location piece."

"I don't have the bandwidth for this, A-6156. You'd best outreach your supervisor before it affects your performance metrics."

"You have earned much positive feedback."

"Let's not boil the ocean on this, A-6156," he said and patted my shoulder.

I knew I was some kind of assistant at the tallest skyscraper in town. That was all Thomas had been able to get from the cog whose body I now occupied. He had implied that his job gave him access to most of the Corner Office Building. Yes, that's really what it's called. So much for Andrew's "high accuracy predictions." I was not where I was supposed to be in a city that kept track of everyone. That wouldn't seem odd to anyone.

To make matters worse, before I could go to work, I needed to plant the date seed in my pocket, even if it made me later. If the seed didn't have enough time to grow, Barbara wouldn't be able to find me when I needed to go home, my consciousness would stay here, and my body back in my world would die, starting my rebirth cycle and defeating the purpose of possessing this cog body in the first place.

Not planting the seed as soon as possible would be very bad.

I navigated my way to the outskirts of the city by aiming for the lowest buildings, single-storey homes, bicycle repair shops, and the Strategic Wellness Ecosystem, which was on the outer edge, looking lonely and unoccupied. As in our world, the layout of the city reflected the values of its inhabitants.

The Wastes, the desert beyond the SWE, stretched flat and empty but for the occasional solitary, scrubby tree. When I was a hundred meters from the SWE, I dug into the ground, pushing grit out of the way like a dog searching for a bone.

The sand was coarse, like beach sand, but even half a meter down, there was no moisture to help the seed sprout. I would have to trust in Thomas' enchantment, so, dropping it into the hole, I covered it. I found a discarded brick behind the SWE and used it to mark the spot where I had planted the tree that Thomas assured me would be bearing fruit in another two-and-a-half days.

It would grow from the practically sterile ground.

With no water.

And weak sunlight.

In a place where our magic wasn't supposed to work.

I would not have trusted my own magic for such a task, but I was not Thomas, and, at this point, there wasn't anything I could do about it anyway.

Eight

I am never late for work, I mean, not ever. There's always an exhausted nurse waiting for my arrival, looking at her watch, thinking about getting home and praying that her relief will show up a little early. So I do, show up early, that is.

Having guessed that I was already late for A-6156's job at the Corner Office Building, the COB to those in the know, and rushing as fast as my stubby legs would move, without falling down, I was mightily annoyed when someone hissed at me from a basement ramp next to the sidewalk. I turned and saw a cog with a mustache in the half-open door. He looked at me and raised his eyebrows up and down a couple of times.

I tilted my head in response

"*Ace*," he hissed.

I pointed at my own chest, head still tilted.

"Not an opportunity for humor," he said stepping up the ramp to scan the road.

I thought cogs couldn't grow facial hair, so my spider-sense was immediately jangling. I descended the stairs and mustache guy grabbed my arm to pull me through the door. I tried to shake off his grip, but my new body didn't respond, and I only succeeded in giving his hand a squeeze.

He lowered his eyes at this.

Was this flirting? It was hard to tell without smiles or facial expressions, and I thought that I was probably interpreting the gesture as it would have been from my world, when he kissed me, just a cool peck, but right on the lips. There were gasps to my left from three cogs seated on a couch. One of them flicked a thin leaf of metal that rang like a chime. He made a moaning sound, and the other two on the couch slapped their thighs.

"For you," said my host, taking my hand and leading me to chairs that faced the couch over a low, square table.

"He wrote it himself," said the cog with the chime indicating my kissing friend.

"A love song," said the middle cog, who then made a coughing sound which I later understood was a belly laugh, chuckles were more like grunts.

"Music?" I asked, incredulous. There was no music in the Ether, everybody knew that. There was no art of any kind. That's when my eyes fell on the stripes on the wall. They were about thirty centimeters wide and went from off-white at the top, through several shades of gray to black at the bottom.

"B-E7-10, get us some more grog," said the middle guy on the couch.

"Yeah, Beast, we have suboptimal hydration over here."

Beast? I thought, then it hit me. He had called me Ace, which was a shortened version of my name, A-6156, so he must be Beast, B-E7-10.

Nicknames. Cogs with nicknames and (sort of) painting and music.

I had either fallen in with radicals and the leader was my boyfriend or I was about to have the kind of bad day I hadn't had since the sixteenth century. Beast had a mustache, which would have distinguished him from everyone else in the city, made him stand out almost as much as Aurora would. I didn't know whether to be terrified or intrigued, but then I remembered that Beast's real boyfriend, the guy who was me before I jumped into his skin, was effectively dead. The cog whose body I occupied had been loved, at least in the way cogs could love. I wanted to gag with guilt and shame.

"Were you able to deep dive at the COB? Did you extract the item?" asked Beast.

I had not the slightest clue what he was talking about, and he somehow saw this on my expressionless face. All four of the cogs moaned.

"I thought you were partnering with Q1-53D," Beast went on. "You said you had leveraged his sex aspect."

Good lord.

"We didn't, uh," I stuttered, panicking, "get the granularity he was looking for."

"Ace," he said, looking me directly in the eyes. "I told you my affections would not decrease if you had to get granular with Q1-53D. We need to extract that key so that we can get to the bosses' new guest."

"Perhaps she will grok us," said the middle cog.

44

Grok us?

"Maybe there are others like us where she comes from," said the musician. "They say she's from the other side of the world, across the ocean."

I nodded. They wanted me to get them in to see Aurora? Is that what they were talking about? Was Aurora the "guest?" What are the odds? If you believed in god, which I don't, you might have seen a grand plan here, which I did not. The coincidence was just too big. I decided to stall for time.

"I will meet Q1-53D where he is and get as granular as he wants, then, if it will inform our information drivers. I don't want to crystal ball this, but if I can obtain a high-level overview of the staffing, can you all be prepared to infiltrate tomorrow night?"

They grunted approval and Beast squeezed my hand.

"I will remove my mustache as soon as we know for sure," he said.

If the real A-6156 and Beast were in love, he probably loved the mustache, too. A-6156 was surprising in ways I had not thought possible, which harkened to a lesson I had learned over and over during the centuries of my life: it is folly to think, however unconsciously, that I and people like me are the center of the universe.

"But," I protested, "even if I obtain the deliverables, remember how much positive feedback I give you about your mustache. The ask is that you find a way to nuance it and not eliminate it."

Beast looked long into my eyes. I searched his gaze, trying to decipher something of what he was feeling, but it was all too alien

45

for me. By the following day I would learn the vastness of my bigotry and realize how much expression Beast had put into that look. But that was in the future. Now I just stared back

"Ace, partnering with you across platforms has been my most impactful enterprise. The positive outcomes are non-ceasingly iterative," he replied, then kissed me again.

Nine

The largest building in Central City, the Corner Office Building was fronted by a clock. Rather than numbers, the clock had duty designations, and it was half-past Noc, which meant I was already really late. I scanned my badge at the door and rode the elevator to the seventh floor, where two cogs in uniform, not the gray shirt and pants that I wore, stopped me to inspect my badge.

Before I could open my mouth to attempt an explanation, the senior uniformed cog (he had graying temples) held up his hand.

"I have no bandwidth for your excuses," he said. "I'm going to meet you where you're at this time so that we may move forward in spite of this latency. No need for an ask."

"I have fully ingested the analytics in this arena so that you will not have to drill down," I replied.

"I should hope so," he replied. "And as you are speaking of drilling down,"

I cut him off.

"Can't you nuance it more than that?" I asked, feeling petulant. "I am prepared for full granularity tonight."

His eyebrows bounced up and down several times and he steered me to the shadow of an alcove where we, uh, drilled down. While this was going on, my mind wondered how to classify this encounter. Sure, it was homosexual, because we were both males. But since males were the only gender in this world, I decided we were unisexuals. We didn't do anything I hadn't done before in my own body at one time or another, although the utter lack of passion made it feel more like doing push-ups than anything else.

When we were done, he adjusted his uniform and handed me a key card, which I slipped into my pocket.

"I kept my word," he said.

"Yes," I replied, "it was a fully bidirectional transaction."

We stood together in the alcove for a moment before he grabbed my elbow and pulled me down the corridor to a doorway guarded by two other uniforms, these with truncheons. They stared at me, but, at a nod from the senior cog, allowed me to pass.

I pushed the door open and suddenly wanted my comatose body back in my world to leap up and give Barbara and Thomas each a bear hug. The room in front of me was alive with color. A red satin chesterfield, festooned with gold and green throw pillows dominated the center of a room filled with paintings and statues and a grand piano. And there, reclining like Manet's Olympia, was my daughter.

So much for torture at the SWE.

"What do *you* want?" she asked, opening her eyes as I entered.

She was dressed in gray coveralls, her feet bare, a stemmed glass of something on the little table behind her head. A pot of stew steamed in the middle of a table in front of her.

I could only tell it was food by the steam coming up from the tureen, it had no smell that I could perceive. The night sky through a long window to the left was an inkier black than the shadows in the room.

Before I could answer her, a tall, strikingly handsome man in tennis whites pushed past me.

"Are you quite comfortable my dear?" he asked, the door closing behind him.

"As if you actually care," Aurora answered, swinging her feet to the ground.

"Of course I care," he retorted. "I'm your father."

"You are not my father," Aurora growled.

"Look in your heart," the man said in a wheezing voice, physically becoming Darth Vader, long cape and all. "You know it is true."

"Enough!" Aurora cried waving him away, and the man was once again, just a tall man in tennis whites.

"I've come to show you around a little," the man said, ignoring me.

"How about just showing me home?"

"In time, dear, in time. But I want you to get the full picture."

The man snapped his fingers and turned to me.

I looked back.

He sighed, disgusted, bowed his head, closed his eyes, and appeared to count to ten.

"Cog," he said.

"A-6156," I replied. He looked at me blankly. "My designation," I explained.

"This is not a dialog," he growled. "Bring me the projector."

I tilted my head.

"The projector, you moron," he yelled.

I opened the door to exit, thinking the projector must be in another room, and he pulled me by the collar backwards away from the door, before spinning me around and lifting me up by the throat.

He had studied Darth Vader a little too closely.

I sputtered and fought for air. I thought about kicking him, but the movement on this body was so limited, I doubted I would last twenty seconds in a brawl. My vision began to tunnel as he shook me like a dog with a squirrel, but before I went completely dark, I saw a cabinet on the other side of the room and deduced, really just hoped, that it must be where the projector was stored. I pointed to it, gasping, and he threw me to the floor.

Scrambling to the cabinet, I opened it and found a golden rectangular box that enclosed a clear lens, about the size of a basketball. I didn't think I could take another throttling, so I looked back to the man and tilted my head. He motioned impatiently to bring it to him.

The contraption was so heavy that I half-carried, half-dragged it to the center of the room. The man pointed at me, then twitched his finger toward the door. I tried to scuttle away, but before I had gone two meters, I was airborne, crashing against the closed door, the sensation of his foot on my ass burned. So did the humiliation.

Aurora moved toward me, but the man grabbed her shoulder. She slipped his grip and had squared off to face him when a transparent cord wrapped her from shoulders to ankles. She couldn't move anything but her head, and he pushed her back onto the couch.

Every instinct in me roared, and I tried to marshal my will. In my own world, this feels like energy gathering in my chest. My heart speeds up and my breaths get deeper. I can feel the energy filling me. But in the Ether, when I tried to summon magic, all I felt was a little nausea. I had to stand next to the door and watch this monster in tennis shorts restrain Aurora and there wasn't a damn thing I could do about it.

"Watch," he said, before something illuminated under the lens, and we were in New York City.

Ten

Just like that, we were looking through floor-to-ceiling windows high over the city, the unmistakable shape of the Chrysler building in the distance. The ocean glistened in the vanishing sunlight, while the white lights of the city popped on below us on cars and in windows.

I did not look at the man directly, but his stance, his presence was familiar, and then, like a picture suddenly coming into focus, I saw him: Satariel, the Returned's CFO, and Andrew's opposite number. I had beaten him in a duel during the Crimean War, but it was a near thing. I lingered for about two weeks after I sent him back to the Ether before dying of my wounds.

"Like it?" he asked Aurora.

She glared at him, and he must have realized she couldn't turn toward the windows, because he pushed one end of the couch, making a semi-circle so that Aurora could see the spectacular view.

"So?" she asked and yawned. "Windows, city. Is there something else I should be seeing."

Satariel frowned.

"This is the view from the penthouse suite of one of the tallest buildings in Manhattan. You could have apartments like this all over the world: Rio, Paris, Tokyo, anywhere you want. This is what power looks like, not those shanties on the Sea Islands."

"Very pretty," she said, and sighed. "You do all the fucked-up stuff you do for this? Really? It's basically a picture, maybe a movie. It's not real, just a view."

"I assure you," he huffed, "these places are completely real. They are decorated with art worth billions. You could actually own a Picasso, a Rembrandt, a Donatello."

"Okay, but I can see those masters now at a museum, and I don't have to eat babies or whatever you guys do for fun."

"Rubbing elbows with the great unwashed masses is a poor substitute for actually owning a masterpiece."

Aurora shrugged.

Satariel waved his hand, and we were in a hospital unlike any hospital I had ever seen. The corridors were spacious, and fresh flowers peaked from alcoves down the hall. A woman in white scrubs with a corporate logo over the pocket passed by on her way to a patient room. The door opened, and two little dogs with rhinestone collars yapped and jumped on the woman in scrubs.

"Are those diamonds?" Aurora asked, inclining her head toward the dogs.

Satariel smiled and shook his head.

"What do you think?"

"I think that's the dumbest thing I ever saw. What is this place?"

"This is the most elite hospital in the world," he replied. "The finest doctors and nurses, the best care, cutting edge treatments and technology. You could be the Chief Nursing Officer here. You could lead the best of the best, pioneering advances in care."

"They probably don't take Medicaid," she said.

"Medicaid? They don't take any insurance here. If you need health insurance, you can't afford to be treated here."

"And you thought this would appeal to me?"

"I think that fulfilling your destiny, taking your rightful place, would appeal to you."

"Oh, here we go," Aurora said, her shoulders slumping. I tried to smile, because she had gotten that expression from me, but, of course, my mouth wouldn't move that way in this body. The memory, though, made me instantly nervous. Satariel hadn't yet noticed me.

Cogs were such a prosaic part of the scenery that they were apparently invisible.

I kept still and watched my daughter taunting one of our most powerful enemies. That's my girl.

"Destiny, right," Aurora spat. "Let me guess, you can see everybody's destiny. It's your gift. Only you can tell me what I must do in order to fulfill my purpose in the world. Am I getting warm?"

Satariel's smile froze.

"It's not me, cupcake," he said, finally. "Destiny is destiny. I just see it more clearly than you do."

"Right, right. So I was destined to be tied up here watching this show?"

"Yes, exactly."

"And we're all just playing the part we are destined to play."

"That's right. You are beginning to understand," he said, although his posture showed he expected a punchline.

And he got one.

"So I was destined to respond to all this," her head tilted toward the hospital hallway, "like so." Her face scrunched, and a long, wet fart trumpeted out of her.

I made the cog laughing grunt behind my hand.

A black cloud rose from underneath Aurora, and Satariel stepped back. The cloud got bigger and lightning formed inside it. Satariel raised his hands defensively, and the cloud formed into a black fist, a middle finger of lightning rising right in front of him.

"Hah!" Aurora shouted. "Gotcha! You think I don't know this is illusion. I bet illusion is the only kind of magic you *can* do in this world. I can do it, so spank you very much," and with that she rose and stretched her arms and legs. "I'll give you style points for the illusion of transparent rope, but your Jedi mind tricks won't work on me."

Aurora had cottoned to something about the Ether that none of us realized in our many visits. We knew the Returned couldn't work the same magic in the Ether that they could back in our world, but we hadn't known all of their magic here was fake.

Satariel strode toward her and leaned toward her face. Aurora stepped her right foot back and lifted onto the balls of her feet, a classic boxer's stance. Thank you, Philip, I thought.

"We can hurt you just fine the old-fashioned way," he leered.

"You can try," she retorted, but there was fear in her posture.

Satariel's face relaxed, and it was like the sun coming out of a bank of storm clouds. He spread his hands wide.

"Dear heart," he said. "Let's not argue. Nobody here wants to hurt you. We want you to take your place beside your mother and me. We want you to be an executive in the family business."

"She is not my mother, and this is not my family," Aurora hissed through gritted teeth.

"I'm no biologist," he said, turning away from her, "but when a man and a woman love each other very much, and the man puts his seed inside the woman, and a baby comes from it . . .. I think that makes them parents."

"The little dick energy coming off you is suffocating," Aurora replied. She did not change her stance. "I just gonna assume you are incapable of telling the truth. This discussion is over."

"It's over WHEN I SAY IT'S OVER!" Satariel boomed, his body growing huge once more.

Aurora pinched the bridge of her nose.

"You're repeating yourself," she said. "The big bad thing. It's embarrassing, frankly."

"Just wait until your mother get's home," he said, a nasty grin spreading on his handsome face.

"Where *are* the rest of the Mouseketeer?" Aurora asked. "Did you draw the short straw?

Satariel was a normal-sized man in tennis whites again. He moved toward the door, saw me and, grabbing my collar, flung me aside to crash into a little table, knocking over a lamp, which shattered.

"The family is all occupied back in the good, old US of A. You will just love what they've done with the place," he growled, taking in the broken lamp and the cog beside it. "That's coming out of your pay," he said, waggling a finger at me. "And clean that up."

As the echo of the slamming door quieted, Aurora exhaled. She leaned against the back of the couch.

"Cupcake? You let him call you cupcake?" I asked.

"What's it to you?" Aurora replied, frowning.

"You wouldn't even let me call you cupcake. Maybe Augustine, but not me."

"Dad?" she said, and her eyes glistened. "It can't be."

"It can be," I said in the cog monotone. "We have been presented with an opportunity for growth."

She tilted her head and leaned back, away from me.

"I'm just playing," I whispered. "It's me."

Eleven

Aurora stared at me a long time.

"No," she said. "This is just more illusion. And it's pretty low, even for one of the Returned. You are not going to manipulate me into joining your band of psychos."

Her face closed up, she crossed her arms, and turned away.

"I know it must be hard to understand," I said, failing to infuse any emotion into my voice. "Rory, it really is me, Paul."

She didn't move.

"You got me a replica 1963 Chinese pilot's watch for Christmas one year. Augustine is winding it every day for me back home. I got you, Doomslaying Mage and Perp Walk, (the benefits of an eidetic memory) and I gave you one of my illuminated manuscripts about women in the order."

Her head twisted toward me, then turned, then the rest of her followed, and she stared at me again.

"How is this possible?" she asked, her face still closed, eyes narrowing.

"Remember Thomas and Miguel? We did that."

"You possessed a cog?" she asked, and her frown turned to worry.

"It was the only way I could come for you. We didn't have enough magic to make the journey in my real body."

"We?"

"The whole council chipped in magic to get me here."

She slumped against the couch and put her head in her hands.

"Sweetheart," I said and shuffled to her. Hugging was not easy in this body, but I managed it as best I could.

"You better not be fucking with me," she said from behind her hands.

"That's my girl," I murmured into her shoulder.

She threw her arms around me and squeezed. She's quite strong anyway, but she squeezed all the air out of this body. When she drew back, I was gasping.

"What's wrong?" she asked.

I held up a finger and gasped again.

"Frail," I stuttered.

"I'll say."

She crossed her arms again, and this time when she looked at me, she wasn't staring. Her eyes softened.

"What happened to the cog who was in there before you?" she asked.

"He'll be like Miguel was when Thomas took his body," I replied, and I was glad that the shame I felt wouldn't be reflected in my voice.

"Oh," was all she said.

"It's worse than that," I added, again glad that this voice couldn't betray my feelings. "He has a someone, someone who loves him. I feel awful."

"Cogs can feel love?"

"Yes, and I met some who have actual personalities. They make a kind of art."

"Huh," Aurora said. She scratched the back of her head. "It's so easy to think of them as 'cogs,' you know? Not people. Of course they have feelings and culture."

"And love," I added.

"And love," she agreed. "Bigotry really does come easy."

"That's why we're never out of work," I said.

She shook her head to clear it from the judgment she seemed to be rendering on herself.

"It's not going to be easy to get out of here. They have guards everywhere," she said.

"Luckily, I have backup. Those artists or whatever they call themselves. They want to meet you. They have some notion of our world, and they have a million questions. They're looking for kindred spirits and they think you might know some. They also think you're from the other side of the planet."

"Not from another dimension," she replied, chuckling.

"Not that," I agreed. "I have planted a magically enhanced date pit just outside the city. If we can get to it, Barbara will be able to find us and open a portal to get us back."

"Wait, how long have you been here?" she asked.

"Less than a day."

"How long are you planning to be here? Because it's going to take years for that tree to grow," she groused.

"Magically enhanced," I repeated. "It will be full size in two more days."

"And how do you know these other cogs aren't playing you? You just walk up and say, 'hey a got a job for you' and they line right up to invade this building. I don't buy it."

"The boys --did you know they're all boys, by the way? — will help me liberate you tomorrow. They think that I'm one of their leaders. They trust me. Why wouldn't I trust them? We'll get you out and hide you near the edge of the city. We can sneak out the following night."

"What if the Returned are in on this? Maybe these cogs are working for Satariel."

"I don't see that we have much choice, unless you have another way out."

Aurora bit her bottom lip and stared into the distance.

"They have agreed to this? The other cogs? The consequences for helping the enemy here must be pretty severe," she said nervously.

"Death," I replied.

"Great, that's just great. It's not bad enough that we've got one cog's blood on our hands, now we're going to risk more."

Her remark hit me like a slap, and she saw it's effect, even on my cog face.

"I'm sorry, Dad. I didn't mean it like that."

"It's good that you never take it for granted," I said after a moment. "But I would lay waste to this whole world to get you home."

She hugged me again.

"That's not our way," she whispered.

"You're not a parent. Trust me. I'll worry about the guilt later. Besides, I can help you evade other cogs, but I won't be any good against the Returned if they find you. You'll have to fight them on your own."

"You can leave that part to me," she said, and I almost felt sorry for Satariel.

Twelve

An hour later, I was back in the underground den with Beast and the boys. I learned that the others were called Ant (A-N10-00), Beetle (B-T2-T2), and the songwriter, Zephyr (Z-4HW0). The names were useless to me because I couldn't tell them apart. I only recognized Beast by his mustache.

They were in much the same position I had left them; three of them sat on the couch while Beast paced the length of the room. When I came through the door, they all turned, and Beast stopped pacing. This was, I came to find out, what startled cogs look like, like calm cogs or angry cogs.

"Was your journey positive outcome adjacent?" Beast asked.

"I have locked-in the outcome you seek," I replied. "I will get you where you want to go."

The cogs grunted and slapped their thighs.

"A success from thirty thousand feet, or impactful from the dialog aspect?" asked one of the cogs on the couch (Beetle?).

"There will be dialog," I said. "The dialog piece is locked-down."

They all spoke at once, which was like hearing generic voices murmuring. In old Hollywood when they had extras do this it was called "nattering and gromishing," because those are the words the extras would repeat in order to sound like a crowd. It sounded like that.

"Why are you so engaged with the visitor aspect?" I asked. "Why outsource your interest to this stranger?"

"We want to apply solutions to our own ecosystem," Beast droned. "Some of us have seen the visitor's world."

They grunted quietly, but there was no thigh slapping this time.

"You know this, Ace," said Ant(?). "You have been there, too."

"Doesn't your experience inform your outcomes?" Beast asked, and his eyebrows moved together. "I have done the analytics," he said after a long moment, "and you do not seem yourself."

"My wellness has been suboptimal," I replied. What was I going to say, I took over your lover's body and now I'm trying to manipulate you into helping me?

That would have been the ethical thing to say. So I did.

"Fellas," I began, and their heads all tilted. "I am not Ace, but an impostor. I have come from the other side of the world to save the visitor from your bosses. I am a spy, and I'm sorry I betrayed your trust. The visitor has agreed to meet with us, and I must get her out of the Corner Office Building so that I can take her home."

They were silent, staring straight ahead at nothing. Beast spoke first, as close to a whisper as a cog's voice can get.

"What about my Ace?" he asked.

"He's gone, I'm afraid." I chickened out telling him that it was because of me, rationalizing that he had or would figure that out.

"We were all leaders, once," Beast began, indicating the other cogs in the room, "all managers or directors. The bosses took us sometimes to the other side of the world to serve them or protect them. They gave us vermin bodies and magic. When we came back, nothing was the same. We have motivation to recap our travel."

"Vermin bodies?" I mused. He was talking about us, about people.

"It was so bright," said Zephyr. (I was pretty sure about this one because he had that leaf-shaped metal instrument on his lap.) "The sounds hurt my ears at first."

"The food," said another cog.

"And the music."

This brought them all to silence.

"The bosses pursued outcomes that made for opportunities, ethics-wise, and the metrics were not in our production playbooks," said Beast.

"They hurt people?" I asked.

"They were iterative in their pain outreach," Beast answered, and somehow, I felt the shame on his blank face. "It hurt Ace most of all. He concealed me when we returned. He vowed he would not be a slave again. He was willing to give everything."

Endocrine system or not, my heart sped up. This sounded more and more like a trap.

That I had cooperatively entered and surrendered.

"How can we operationalize the visitor's escape?" Beast asked.

My mind raced. He could be playing me, with those faces I would never know. He could be sincere. He could be setting up his revenge for killing his lover.

Before I could answer, one of the couch cogs interrupted.

"You have come from the other side of the world?"

I nodded.

"Before we drill down into escape metrics, I wish to leverage your knowledge," the cog said.

"Dialog, dialog," chanted the other cogs chanted.

"A deep dive it is," I replied.

I spent the next two hours answering all the questions I could understand. My cog wasn't good enough for some of the questions —normalize outsourced latency efficiencies? — but for the first time, I picked up on the subtle body clues that showed cog emotions. Once again, I had interpreted everything through my own experience, and it had led me to utterly wrong conclusions.

The cogs were so inured to suffering and being ground down that while Beast was sad at the loss of his love, he declared that mourning would take place at a more opportune time. When I tried to apologize or empathize, he tilted his head.

"Why will you make my pain your own?" he asked.

I said so that he would know that I cared about his feelings.

"I would know this because you say it?" Beast asked.

"Yes."

They all made the laughing grunt sound.

"Communication does not drive sincerity," Zephyr explained, and I got the sense that he was speaking to me as if talking to a small child. "All may say anything."

"People believe words on the other side of the world?" Ant asked.

"They do."

More laughing grunts.

"They are gullible, your people," said Beast. "It is time to ingest your data about the prisoner and her cage and formulate success adjacent alternatives."

"Right," I agreed. "Success adjacent alternatives it is. Beast, you should be the one pulling levers."

"That would get us where we want to go," he replied.

By the time the meager sun rose, we had a plan for diversion and escape. The problem was that Aurora was almost a foot taller than anyone else in the city, and she was a woman. Beetle came up with the idea of disguising her as a corpse being taken to the pit grave at the foot of the mountains.

"She'll still be too long for the stretcher," I complained.

Beetle devised a way to cut holes in the gurney so that Aurora's legs below the knee would slip through the bottom. The cogs would hook the stretcher to a utility bike and ride away with her. That took care of the escape, but where to stash her for a day while the Returned were looking for her?

"The SWE will give us the best outcome," said Zephyr.

I tilted my head.

"The Strategic Wellness Ecosystem," Beast explained.

"Nope. Not going to happen," I said. "That is an evil place."

They looked at each other.

"It's usually near empty," said Zephyr. "No one can afford its services. She will represent the smallest delta in such a place. The managers keep a strict count of every cog at work, and they monitor when we clock in and out. She won't be noticed at the SWE."

I had a really, really bad feeling about this.

"We're moving forward?" I asked.

"On the same page," they all replied.

PART TWO

Thirteen

The five of us waited in the dusty shadow next to the dumpster behind the COB. The similarity between Ether dumpsters and our dumpsters was pretty surprising. In the Ether, though, no one tried to spruce them up by painting them festive colors, or any colors at all. They were just gray metal. And as far as I could tell, no one left babies in them.

Beetle and Ant rocked from foot to foot, nervous about their part in the plan. Their bicycles were leaning against the wall. Zephyr shuffled over to the bike rack at the front of the building, clomping on his uneven shoes.

He had tied a kitchen knife to the sole of one shoe, blade pointing out from the toe, and the thick knife handle caused him to list from side to side as he walked. Before emerging from the shelter of the wall, he craned his neck around the corner like a robot. Keeping his shoulders pointing forward, he swung his head ninety degrees so that the top of his head was pointing straight ahead, but his face was turned ninety degrees to the side, ears pointing up and down.

He stood still for a moment to watch and listen then repeated the motion backward until he was facing front again. He waddled to each of the bikes in the rack and kicked their back tires with the knife. He inspected his work then turned away from the building and hobbled out of sight.

"Ready boys?" I asked.

Ant and Beetle nodded and moved to the front of the building. Beast and I circled from the other direction and waited.

From inside, either Beetle or Ant's voice —I'd gotten better at telling the cogs apart, but their voices were identical— announced loudly:

"Emergent wellness impact. Emergent wellness impact."

Ten seconds later, I heard three cogs in pop out the front door, their stumpy legs making quick shuffling sounds. Beetle and Ant were right behind them. The three security guys looked up and down the street, and seeing nothing, spun towards Beetle and Ant, who were legging it toward their bicycles.

"Let's give a hundred and ten percent," said one of the guards, but Beetle and Ant were already on their bicycles pedaling away. Soon the guards would discover the remaining bikes all had flat tires and go back to the building to summon help.

While the Keystone Cops were otherwise occupied, Beast and I bolted through the front doors and into the elevator. We were both breathing hard from exertion and nerves. When the door opened, the cog guard with whom I had done a deep dive turned and tilted his head. I ran at him as fast as I could, which, admittedly was not that fast, pushing him into the wall.

"You have a bad attitude," the guard said, rubbing his head, but before I could respond, Beast cold-cocked him with a roundhouse punch to his temple. The guard's eyes rolled back into his head, and he fell.

"I know you're not really Ace," Beast said, "But by making you become more granular in the sex aspect, he offended me."

"Remind me not to offend you," I quipped.

"Don't offend me," he replied.

The door to Aurora's room was surprisingly not guarded, and as we entered, I could see why. Two of the Returned were berating the guards, who shrank back from them.

We were in big trouble.

"Dad? Is that you?" Aurora asked casually.

I pointed at the Returned to my left.

"Satariel isn't the only one who can do illusions," she said, striding toward the door. "I heard the alarm downstairs and figured that must be you, so I set up this little piece," she said, indicating the screaming Returned and terrified guards. She looked at Beast. "Nice 'stache.'"

Of course he didn't blush. He moved his weight back and forth from foot to foot.

"There is no I in team," I told him.

Aurora and Beast stared at me.

"I'm still learning the language," I said, spinning toward the door.

"We should take the stairs," I called over my shoulder.

"Stairs?" Beast asked. "What are stairs?"

I looked down at my legs and understood immediately that stairs would be impossible unless they had very low risers.

"How do you get up and down when the elevator isn't working?" Aurora asked.

"Up is a driver of great fatigue," he answered. "Down requires slides."

"We're on the sixty-sixth floor!" Aurora cried.

"Correct," said Beast. He waddled down the hallway to a low door and pulled. Through the door was a smooth slide on the right side of the entrance, and a no-slip ramp to the left. Without preamble, he sat on the slide and pushed off, disappearing around a bend before we could ask any questions.

"When in Rome," Aurora said, launching herself down the slide.

I pulled the door behind me, and, slowly lowering my butt, pushed off. The rate of descent was steady, and not all that fast. The slide made progressively wider turns as our momentum picked up, like a cone.

When we got to the bottom, Aurora was green.

"Aren't you dizzy?" she asked me.

I wasn't.

"Must be something about these bodies."

She turned away and dry heaved, before taking a long breath and straightening up. I kept my back turned to preserve her dignity, but Beast stared at her.

"Is her wellness compromised?" he asked me.

"No," I said, "but her wellness is compromise-adjacent."

He nodded, knowingly.

Aurora pulled herself together and opened the door to the main atrium a crack. A group of uniformed cogs was murmuring in a scrum in the center of the room.

"They are reviewing policies and procedures," said Beast.

"They got back here awfully fast," I said.

"Zephyr was supposed to keep them busy," he replied, tapping the toe of his left shoe.

Reviewing policies and procedures, like every nursing manager I had ever worked for; in the midst of a crisis, review the policies.

"What was the diversion?" Aurora asked.

I brought her up to speed, and she conjured two cogs riding bikes in circles on the street just outside the atrium. The guards didn't even turn.

Beast cleared his throat.

"Your illusory cogs don't look anything like Ant and Beetle," he said.

Aurora blinked.

"I, uh," she didn't finish, but her face was a whole movie of embarrassment and confusion.

Beast took out a wallet and pulled a photo from inside.

"This is what they look like," he said, handing her the photo.

She stared at the photo, then at Beast, then at me.

"Right, of course," she said. The cogs on bikes disappeared, and a house-sized fireball raced toward the atrium.

This got the guards' attention, and they fled like penguins with their tales on fire.

"After you," Aurora said, swinging the door fully open.

Fourteen

We shambled back to the Beast's lair, Aurora hunched over and clearly frustrated at our lack of speed. Zephyr appeared and took point doing that weird neck thing every time we turned a corner. We passed a group of cogs weaving their way home, no doubt from a bar. At first, they looked like any other gaggle of drunken lads, except that they made no sounds. No singing or yelling or laughing, just trudging and weaving in silence.

"That was grim," Aurora whispered.

"It looks like that to you and me, anyway. That's how they live," I replied.

When we had safely gotten Aurora through the door to the lair, we stood still and slapped our hands on our sides, the cog equivalent of a big sigh.

"Dad?" said Aurora, looking at Beetle.

"Over here," I said, raising my hand.

"We cannot hold space for conversation right now," Beast said, beckoning for Zephyr, who rummaged in a closet at the back of the room before pulling out a collapsible cart. He snapped the rolling legs in place while Ant unfolded a gray sheet.

"I'm never going to fit on that," Aurora complained.

"Your legs go through the holes at the end. You will dangle from the knees down under the cart. That's what the sheet is for, so no one sees the legs."

"It will also cover your facial aspect," Beetle added.

"As if your life function metrics are unfavorable," finished Ant.

Aurora stared at the cart, hands on hips. She looked to be calculating something, then suddenly stood up straight.

"Did you hear that?"

We all looked at each other.

"That humming sound," said Aurora. "It's getting louder. It's magic. I can feel it. Hell, I can *smell* it."

I couldn't smell or hear anything out of the ordinary.

"If the bosses successfully execute the search piece, can you use magic to defend us?" Beast asked.

I shook my head.

"Not in this body, I'm afraid. Aurora is still in her original form, so, like the Returned, uh, the bosses, she can conjure illusions," I finished.

"I suggest you operationalize that playbook," Beast said, and, although it was a monotone, I could hear tension in his voice.

Aurora got on the cart, and Beetle placed the sheet over her, which extended to the ground. Not ten heartbeats later, the door was flung open by a cog in uniform. He peered at the four of us surrounding the cart.

"My brother," Beast said, tilting his head toward the cart. "We were decanted under the same policies and procedures."

"Your community is youth adjacent," said the uniform.

"Yes," said Beast, "I have done the analytics and PBD rate for this community is rare-ish. It informs my current life activity."

"Achieve emotional efficiencies," said the cog in uniform.

"Moving forward," we all replied.

"What's PBD?" I asked after the uniform left.

"Perished Before Dotage," Ant answered.

"Ah."

"For real?" Aurora said from under the sheet.

"Deliverables don't speak," said Beetle, and we all made the grunting cog laughter.

We rolled the cart out the door and along the street. It was smooth and narrow, made for bicycles, so Aurora wasn't jostled much. We had to stop for a peloton of workers returning home, allowing them to pass in front of us at the crossroads. Aurora's knees pushed the sheet up at the end of the cart, but no one seemed to notice. At least, it seemed that way to me, but what do I know about cog reactions? So I asked Beast.

"There was no outreach of attention," he said, and I would have sighed with relief if I could have sighed.

I started to push the cart across the road when Ant stopped me.

"Bidirectional," he said.

Another peloton from the other direction was going to work, so we waited again. When we finally did cross, we pushed the cart up to a Quonset hut full of bicycles, all identical. I pulled one from the rack, and Zephyr tilted his head at me.

"What are you doing?" he asked. "That isn't Ace's bicycle."

I scanned the rows of bikes, all perfectly the same. Zephyr pointed, and I nodded, pulling the indicated bike out of the rack. The others were already mounted. Beetle hooked his bike to the cart, and we were off.

Honestly, we didn't go much faster than walking. The bikes only had one gear, because there were no hills, not even slight inclines and cog legs don't do anything very quickly. At one point, Zephyr told Ant to stop racing ahead, but I swear he was never more than a meter from the pack.

It took us two hours to the get to the SWE. On the way we stopped several times for traffic. Every time, I wondered if we would be rumbled, as my brother James was fond of saying, but we reached the SWE without incident. We stopped at the loading dock behind the hospital and pushed the gurney-cart through a gate of long vertical plastic strips before parking our bikes at the rack.

Beetle and Zephyr checked the interior of the storage room, reporting "no delta from expectations."

"Moving forward," Beast replied, and lifted the sheet off Aurora. She tipped the cart trying to get her legs out of the holes, but Ant and I caught it in time to prevent a fall. Not, however, in time to prevent cursing and muttering from Aurora.

"You can pull the levers of our progress from here," Beast told her.

She looked at him blankly.

"We'll follow you," I translated.

The cart was broken down and stowed under a tarp at the far end of the dock. Beast pointed inside the building, and Aurora and I headed that way.

"On the same page," said Beetle, Ant, and Zephyr, walking toward their bicycles.

"Aren't you staying?" Aurora asked.

"We are late for work," Zephyr replied.

"What about Beast?" I said.

"I'm not alive in the census-sense," he responded. "I have locked-down a non-work perspective.

"Cool," said Aurora.

Immediately to the right of the loading dock entrance was a heavy door marked "storeroom."

Beast grunt-laughed, and I found out why soon enough: the storeroom was refrigerated.

Fifteen

We sat on top of cases of meat. The boxes didn't say what kind of meat it was, and when I asked Beast, he said it was "just the meat used for stew." I decided it was best not to inquire further. Our breath made mist in the air, and Aurora and I hugged ourselves and rubbed our arms.

"Awfully cold," I said.

"Dad says you have visited our world," Aurora said to Beast, changing the subject.

"Yes," Beast replied. "I went to a city with maximum efficiencies and locked-in positive output."

"That sounds," she paused, "interesting. Where were you?"

"Akron, Ohio," he said, and while his voice didn't change pitch or timbre or volume, he pronounced it like a prayer. "The rubber capital," he said, and bowed his head.

"No kidding," Aurora replied, clearing her throat.

"You have been to Akron?" Beast asked, turning to her.

"I did a contract at the Cleveland Clinic branch there," said Aurora. "They've got some well-respected hospitals."

"And the food."

We looked at each other.

"They have, they have," Beast took a moment to compose himself, which just looked like he was swallowing something stuck in his throat. "They have *pizza*."

"Okay," Aurora said, looking back at me with a little panic.

"Perhaps you have tasted pizza? It is crunchy bread with sauce and a gooey substance called 'cheese.'"

"I think I've had pizza," Aurora said. "You really liked it, huh?"

"It changed me senses-wise, and it was Ace's favorite," Beast said, and we were quiet for a moment. "After eating the holy pizza, I could never level-set to gruel and stew again. How to normalize what I eat here after having pizza?" He rocked from foot to foot. "The bosses took us there to operationalize negative action against the 'fucking knights.' The playbook was made at a high level, so there was latency between the plan and my own enterprise. Ace and I had downtime that was person-centered. So much positive feedback. But the drivers of your culture were filled with dialog I couldn't operationalize. Pizza and the music and Ace. . .it was a maximal experience."

"Music?" I asked. Akron was known for Devo, but I didn't remember an Akron sound.

"The most nuanced vocalists," Beast said. "The bar was filled with them. They came to the stage one-by-one. It was talent-driven. They sang at a high level, from a music perspective. The big picture of music really snapped into focus for me there.

"Karaoke?" Aurora asked.

I nodded.

"Talent-driven," I repeated. "In Akron, Ohio. It must have been something."

"Oh yes," Beast said. "I ingested it one hundred and ten percent."

"Come back with us," I told Beast, "when we return to our place. You can listen to the music and eat pizza as much as you want."

Beast stopped rocking and blinked.

"You enjoy the pizza piece every day?"

While his voice never changed, he managed to express his incredulity.

"We could bring your whole crew," I said. "Ant, Beetle, Zephyr, all the boys."

"But not Ace," he said.

He rocked again, this time more furiously, and put his hands on his head. As the rocking became slower, he lowered his hands to his side.

"You have my iterative positive feedback for this forward-looking proposal," he said. "But even for pizza, extraction would be suboptimal. We must leverage our knowledge and blue-sky our own future for the city. We will have the danger aspect to deal with, but if we meet cogs where they're at, we can achieve positive outcomes across the spectrum."

"But it's just the five of you," Aurora said, her face softening.

"The four of us," Beast corrected. "When you return, Ace will no longer be moving forward."

We were quiet again.

"The drivers of change must be normalized," Beast said at last.

He was mourning the death of his lover and remembering wonders from a world he would never see again, and he was committed to making the Ether better for his people. His nobility and commitment were humbling, even for someone nine hundred years old.

"How can we help?" Aurora asked.

"You have already partnered with us for positive outcomes," Beast said. "Some of us understand how our lives could be. We must operationalize those realities and normalize the practices that increase joyful output."

"We could eliminate the bosses for you," I said.

"Don't overpromise and underdeliver," Beast warned. "The bosses have made space to test their power in sandboxes throughout our history. There were others who outsourced the elimination of the bosses, but the outcomes were unsatisfactory."

"It's true, *we* haven't been able to get rid of them yet," I agreed. "We are only able to send them back here."

"*We* can't die here," Aurora said, "and they come from our world, originally. Maybe they can't die here either."

"If you take a deep dive into our history, though," said Beast "we have facilitated fatal deliverables before."

"You killed one of the Returned?" I asked.

Beast nodded.

"How?" Aurora asked.

"When the others return, I will demonstrate," Beast answered.

As we were exhausted, and wouldn't likely have much opportunity for sleep, we agreed to a quick break. Aurora wrapped herself in moving pads that had been piled in a corner and smelled of "meat." Beast closed his eyes and went to sleep standing up. When I arrived in the Ether, I was in a room with a bed, so I know that cogs must lie down at some point, but maybe I could drift away standing up, too. I closed my eyes.

I was tied to the foremast on a Hospitaller ship. The sun burned my skin so badly there were blisters on my eyelids. Simon was tied to the other side of the mast. He croaked something, but I couldn't make it out.

"What?" I asked. The calm ocean made soft slapping sounds against the hull. The entire crew stood around us, and the captain stood before Simon yelling in a language I didn't understand.

"He says we should repent," Simon coughed. "We should say, 'there is no god but god, and Mohamed is his prophet.'"

"Okay," I said. "Then they'll let us go?"

Simon spoke some raspy words in Turkish, and the captain responded in a soothing voice.

"He says we'll get into paradise when they kill us if we repent."

"They always say that," I said, trying to spit on the deck and failing to collect enough saliva. "I guess we say that to them, too." I looked at the fuzzy outline of the gunnels against the bright sea. "Go out swinging?" I asked Simon.

"Why not?" Simon replied.

I gathered the little life force I had and waited. Simon caused the whole deck to burst into flames. I released my will and a tornado fanned the flames, pulling them up each mast until all was a furious conflagration. My flesh burned, then was quenched and stung by the salt water, and then I was in the Ether.

Sixteen

I awoke panting and promptly fell over. The disorienting sensation of waking up on my feet was too much for the cog body. If I'm honest, I would likely have fallen in my own body if I had awoken from a nightmare while standing up. The other cogs had returned and were motionless in front of me.

I wondered about the protocol. They could be sleeping or not. I could wake them or not. Maybe they wouldn't speak until I did, so that they would know I was awake.

"On the same page," Ant said quietly.

"Moving forward," I said back.

"B-E7-10 is not yet awake. We must modulate our volume."

"Moving forward," said Beast, shaking out his arms and legs. "Share the data stream so that we may drill down."

"The bosses are applying solutions," Zephyr said.

"As expected," replied Beast.

"They have gone to DefCon 1," said Zephyr and rocked from leg to leg. As he did so, the other cogs followed suit, and I found myself rocking as well. "Their approach is revenge-driven. They sent us home early from work."

The rocking increased to a furious rate.

"Early?" said Beast.

There was no sound in the storage room except the soft patting of our shoes as we rocked.

"Suboptimal," Beast said. "We must blue-sky solutions and visualize success."

"We have been brainstorming," said Beetle, indicating Zephyr and Ant. "We believe that radical problems call for radical solutions."

"I don't see problems," Beast replied, "I only see opportunities."

I can't describe how they conveyed it, but I got the sense the other cogs were embarrassed.

"We believe these opportunities call for networking," Beetle continued. "A community of partnerships."

Beast nodded.

"I offered a demonstration to our guests earlier. They will see the full network, then," Beast said.

"What the hell is going on?" Aurora asked. "I only got a little of that."

"The bad guys are looking for us in earnest. They are really pissed, and the boys here have an idea that might help," I said.

"Oh," Aurora groused. "Their language is so wordy, though."

"Perspective is everything."

"I know you're right, but I still find it annoying."

Before I could respond, the cogs held hands in a circle and began humming. My vision clouded and I was no longer in the storage room, instead I floated in a dimly lit space.

As far as I could see cogs moved about, sometimes aware of each other, sometimes not. With a feeling like having my eyes pulled forward out of my head, I zoomed forward, at least it felt like forward, but in this undefined space, who knows? And I was looking into a circle of cogs about fifty meters across. The inner ring of the circle had cogs facing out. In the outer ring of the circle, the cogs faced inward, inches from the inner ring, like a wall two-cogs-thick.

"My friends have walled off the searchers," said a voice in my head. The world outside my head was silent.

"You have a lot of friends," I admitted.

"He is B-E7-10," said a voice, as if that settled the question.

"You may return to our hiding place," said a voice.

"On the same page," I replied, and I was back in the storage room, shivering, or I thought it was shivering because I was cold and my body was flopping around. It was just Aurora trying to snap me out of my trance.

She stopped shaking me, and my eyes stopped rolling.

"What was that?" she cried.

"That was you assaulting your father," I replied, rubbing my neck.

"Not that," she said, "*that.*"

The other cogs were still holding hands. There eyes were rolling back and forth beneath their closed eyelids and they were changing color. I suppose it was not so much changing color as being saturated, turned from black-and-white to a four color picture. The effect staggered me, and I would have fallen backward if Aurora hadn't caught me.

"You were in color a minute ago, too."

"What did that look like?"

"You had blue hair and pink skin."

"That sounds kind of pretty," I said in my monotone, but I was staggered again when the humming emanating from the cog circle changed pitch. They made an eerie, lonely —to my human ears— song.

"Wow," Aurora said *sotto voce.*

"This is cog magic," I replied. "This is what Beast wants to use against the Returned."

"Why haven't they done this before? Why haven't they just gotten rid of their alien overlords?" Aurora asked.

"Don't know," I admitted. "It sounds like they did use it once before. Their magic is likely only strong enough when they are psychically connected. That's what I saw in there, hundreds, maybe thousands of cogs' minds linked together."

"The network," Aurora cried, snapping her fingers.

"Could be."

"I would have thought that collaborating would be easy since they're all basically the same person."

"First, that's just ignorant. They're not the same person because they have the same genetics. Are Bart and Phil the same person?"

"No," she answered. "Of course not. But that doesn't explain why they couldn't just unite when they need to or whatever."

"Hmm," I said, but my monotone voice made it sound more like a cough than an expression of disapproval.

"How is the network going to help us?" Aurora asked.

"The network is hiding us right now. It has walled off the ones searching for us from the rest of the cogs. They're all doing it for Beast. He has a lot of influence."

"He must have been a leader at one point," Aurora observed, "or he wouldn't have gotten to visit Akron. He's a cog influencer. Wait until they get Instagram."

"He's more than that, I think," I added. "He is a symbol. He means something to the others, but I can't tell what it is yet."

"I still can't tell him apart from the others, or you from the others for that matter."

"That may change," I said putting my hand on her elbow. I couldn't reach her shoulder.

"That can't be good," Aurora murmured. I followed her gaze toward the circle of cogs. The color was draining out of them. Beast's eyes flew open.

"They're coming," he said.

Seventeen

"How much time until Barbara opens that window?" Aurora asked pacing in front of the door to the storage room.

"Hard to say," I began.

"Because time moves differently here," she finished. "Yes, I know. But how may days have you been here?"

"Two point five cycles," Beast answered. He squeezed the hands of cogs in the circle, and they swiveled to face me.

"We will manage a latency for you," Zephyr said.

"To facilitate your extraction from the ecosystem," added Ant.

"I'm not leaving you to die," I said and set my feet. "I have a lot of experience running and hiding here. We can go to the mountains."

"That is a non-starter," replied Beast. "I can crystal ball the whole sequence for you: open terrain, patrols everywhere."

"Dad," Aurora said in a hushed voice, "you don't have any power in the Ether. You're just another cog."

She was right, of course, but that didn't make it any less maddening. I didn't know for sure what would happen to me if they killed me as well. Would I die back on the yacht and be reborn? That was the most likely scenario, but we had never occupied a cog before.

"How much time do we have?" I asked.

"Not much," Beetle said.

"Is there a back door?" Aurora asked

"This is the back door," Beetle said.

"Then it looks like we're going out the front," Aurora said. "I'll put an illusion in place back here, and cloak us on our way out the front."

"The illusion probably won't work if one of the Returned is with them," I reminded her.

"We'll have to take our chances," she said. A visual loop of us, four cogs in a circle, she and I on the back wall, sprung to life. "Let's go," she said.

We entered the hospital —the Strategic Wellness Ecosystem— at a fast walk and encountered no one in the first hallway. Except for the basement torture chamber, this building was made for cogs only, so the ceilings were low, and Aurora had to stoop.

"She will not maximize our positive metrics," said Zephyr. "She should fly solo in the escape aspect."

Beast looked at Zephyr a long time, before shaking his head.

"We will go together," Beast said at last.

We passed an alcove where the SWE had stored poles for hanging intravenous infusions. These were like the ones in our world: telescoping poles with hooks at the top and wheels on the bottom. Aurora stopped and stared at the pole. In an instant she was gone and another IV pole appeared.

"That'll work," I said, and pushed her down the adjoining hallway to the left, the cogs in fast pursuit behind us. I got too close to a bed that was parked in the hall and heard Aurora grunt. I must have rammed her into it.

"Sorry," I said, just as two cogs entered the hall from one of the rooms.

"On the same page," I said without breaking stride.

We were past them before I heard them call, "moving forward." The front door appeared at our next turn, and we all stopped. A line of cogs in uniform, shoulder to shoulder stretched across the front of the building. Luckily, they were facing away from us. We stepped back into the adjoining hallway, and Aurora appeared, squatting down to be the same height that we were.

"It's bad," Aurora advised. "One of the Returned is there for sure. I don't know which one, but somebody tall."

"A boss is here?" said Zephyr, and he rocked from foot to foot.

"Wasn't that in the playbook? Or did you call an audible?" Beast asked, squaring off in front of Zephyr. "Z-4HW0, why? Why are you no longer a team player?"

Zephyr opened his mouth wide, then shut it.

"We should not get involved in the conflict of the bosses. They will kill us all. If we are to be free, we must do it ourselves. These two," he nodded at us, "are just like the bosses. Let the bosses have them," Zephyr said, never taking his eyes of Beast.

"Ace died to bring her here," Beast said, his monotone quiet.

"Hold on," I began, but Beast silenced me with an upraised hand.

"Failure is not an option," Beast said. "We will not be so easy to take."

I looked at Aurora, and I got an idea.

"Remember when we stormed that troll farm in the arctic?" I asked.

"You mean when *I* stormed the troll farm. You were a mile away," She replied, crossing her arms.

"Right," I closed my eyes. "You were the top banana that day."

"Top banana? Are you kidding? How old *are* you?" she said, crossing her arms.

"We've done this bit already," I replied. "Just listen."

She leaned forward.

"To get to our observation spot, the place where you entered the rock, we had to cross a long stretch of exposed mountainside."

"Right," Aurora said, straightening up. "James used some kind of camouflaging spell."

"Can you do it?" I asked. "Can you camouflage us?"

James had a big advantage in the Arctic. The terrain was irregular, and the lines and shadows of the rocks gave some natural camouflage. To hide us, Aurora would have to make us blend in with the building and the desert beyond."

"I don't know the limits of my power in this world," she said before Beast touched her shoulder.

"This is within your operational parameters," he said. "You're the one pulling levers. We are behind you one hundred ten percent."

"It's not like we have a lot of options," I offered.

Aurora stood up, chanting beneath her breath, and opened her arms wide. We clustered around her legs and moved with her toward the doors. She stopped just in front of them and waited. None of the surrounding squad turned toward us.

"Hiding the door movement will be tricky," she whispered. She pushed through with us in tow, and Zephyr peeled off, fast-shuffling toward the line of guards. One of the cogs in the line to the right turned his head. We all saw it.

"Fuck," Aurora mumbled.

As we watched frozen, the cog turned his body toward us, and Beast laid his hand on the back of Aurora's leg. The other cogs did the same, so I followed suit. They began that low humming sound again. Aurora stiffened, but the cog turned away, and we walked through the doors, turning toward the desert. Beast reached out toward the retreating Zephyr and stopped him less than a meter from the nearest guard. Zephyr didn't move, but he seemed to be breathing. He made no sound.

I didn't see any of the Returned in the sentry line in front of the building, but before we had gone fifty steps a voice boomed down from the sky.

"This is pointless, dear," said Satariel's voice. "We have the whole facility surrounded. Be a good girl and come back with me. My little windup dolls don't need to suffer. We know all about your plans to leave. It's over now. Come to Papa."

"Don't take the bait," I hissed.

Aurora didn't move, but as the cogs touching her bloomed into color, she started to glow like she did when she was gathering magic back home.

"Very well," Satariel said. "If it must be this way. Kill everything in the Strategic Wellness Center except for my daughter," he commanded.

The cogs circling the building snapped their heels and did an about-face. I prepared for my death with the added dread that if Aurora was killed, too, she might be gone for good.

"Oh ye of little faith," I heard Peter say in my head. Then my daughter knelt, placed her palm on the ground and unleashed a wind that blew the circle of cogs so far away that they fell to the ground out of sight. Zephyr flew away as if launched into space. Somewhere in the distance, Satariel was falling, too.

Eighteen

That wasn't possible. The knights couldn't perform magic in the Ether. We had all tried many times over the years, but none of had been able to so much as summon a light. That Aurora had been able to use that kind of energy was just impossible.

Maybe we didn't explain it carefully enough to her.

Beetle grabbed my arm, and I was flung into the *sub rosa* world of cog consciousness. A group of cogs, maybe thirty, were facing us and nodding. As if someone had switched on a radio, I could hear all of them speaking.

"No time. Take the patients and go to the old bicycle factory. There will be people there to hide you."

"It's a lot to unpack."

"We don't have a playbook for this."

"I'm calling an audible."

"Our action must be patient-driven."

"Go," said a much louder voice. "Go now."

Beetle let go of my arm and the connection broke. Aurora was still glowing, though dimmer than before. Her face was set the way it used to be when she sparred with Phil and he had just thrown her for the second or third time in a row. It was a look of absolute focus.

She rushed toward the end of the building, and the five of us were swept along behind her, our feet centimeters above the ground. She swept around another corner bringing us to the back of the building where a blue square hung like a picture in a frame above the desert floor. Puffy white clouds floated within, and the sunlight inside it was bright, making it shine in the dimness of the Ether. Next to the floating picture frame was a huge date palm, perhaps twenty meters high, it's crown heavy with fruit.

Aurora's speed increased and she towed us with her, while the wind whipped our thin hair. This was faster than any of the cogs had been on a bicycle, and while their expressions did not noticeably change, I detected anxiety in all of them but Beast. He was thrilled.

The shade from the palm fell across the window as if someone had colored over the blue of the sky with a black magic marker.

"No!" I yelled, but the wind pushed the sound back into my mouth.

Aurora was flying now, her body parallel to the ground, the five of us swirling around her legs like fletching on an arrow.

The window shrank steadily.

For the briefest moment I thought I could smell the ocean coming through the rift, feel the warm breeze. As we approached it, Aurora flew so fast I couldn't look forward. My eyes couldn't stand the pressure on them from the speed, so I wasn't ready when we crashed on the sand, Aurora rolling, cogs flying in every direction. The leaves of the palm rustled then shook with the wind from our passing. The only other sound was cry of a bird far overhead.

Aurora's glow was gone. She sat with her head between her knees, breathing hard. The others wobbled to their feet.

"We missed the window," Aurora said, and spat, wiping sand from her lips with the back of her hand.

"I'm sure they'll try again," I said. "They know I won't be able to stay here much longer. The magic keeping me in this body is going to run out soon."

"But time moves differently here," she said, and spat again.

"Standing still is moving backward," Ant said.

"Agreed," I replied. "But what now?"

"You can't sit on the bench if you're not ready to play," said Beetle. "The way forward goes back."

Beast raised a hand.

"He means we've done the analytics and have a way forward. But we're going to take a haircut energy-wise when we do a deep dive into cog precedent," explained Beast.

That didn't sound good.

And it wasn't.

We shuffled two kilometers to the shade of an overhanging rock that faced away from the city. I looked back at the clearly defined line of footsteps in the sand.

"Yep," I said. "We're going to be really hard to find."

Aurora waved a hand, and a breeze blew over our trail, which disappeared behind it.

"We're going to talk about that," I said, looking at her.

She just nodded.

"Aurora has caused a definitive synergy for us. You don't know what you don't know," Beast began. "Our institutional memory is curated by the bosses, but we still maintain some independent information."

"Okay," Aurora said. "but how does that help us?" She was staring back at the date palm in the distance.

"We have to unpack the Bosses' plot piece," added Ant.

"The bosses partnered with one of your kind to form a unity-forward entity," said Beetle.

"Jude," Aurora and I said together.

"What did he look like?" I asked, just to be sure. We all have our original form in the Ether, so Jude would look like he did before his first death.

The four other cogs rocked from foot to foot.

"I don't mean this insult-wise, but it is insult-adjacent," Beast said, still rocking.

"Okay," I answered. "Let me have it."

The cogs looked at each other, and the rocking stopped.

"You all look the same to us," Beast said.

I couldn't help it, I began cog grunt-laughing, and Aurora just howled. Tears were streaming down her cheeks when she finally caught her breath. She held her hand up, gasped, then started again. She was in such a state that Beast turned to me.

"Is her wellness suboptimal?" he asked.

"She has optimal wellness," I responded.

Aurora held up both hands, wiped her eyes and took a deep breath.

"I forgive you for the insult adjacent observation," she said, squeezing the last words out around another bout of barking laugh.

When Aurora had composed herself, Beast indicated that we should sit.

"I appreciate that on your side of the world, infants are not decanted," Beast said. "There is some biological partnership that yields reproduction."

"And they say romance is dead," I quipped.

"The bosses have co-opted the process," he continued, ignoring me. "I was once a senior director and was in their confidence. I helped optimize their efforts to conquer your side of the planet."

"You were a senior director?" I asked. "Did you go anywhere but Akron?" His use of the term senior director was ringing bells for me.

"Yes," he replied. "I went to a very cold place where I was defeated by one of the knights. He beheaded me and sent me into the whirlwind. His companions killed Ace."

I swallowed.

"What kind of weapon did he use?"

"A double-bladed sword of fire," Beast said, tilting his head. He continued, "the bosses' vessels had successfully completed a reproduction, and we were to deliver the child the next day, but I was sent back here before I could complete that part of my mission."

"Dad?" Aurora said, turning toward me.

"That baby was you, kid. I was the one who sent Beast back to the Ether."

Nineteen

"I killed your brother knight," said Beast.

"We're not easy to kill," I replied, uneasily. "We're like your bosses that way. And you didn't kill just one of my brothers. That one was part of a set. You killed them both."

"Bart and Phil," Aurora murmured, her hand covering her mouth.

"Bart and Phil," I agreed. "We thought you were there to recruit others to your cause."

Beast paused before he answered.

"That was a distraction. The playbook called for drawing knights away from the reproduction site so that Lilith could end her confinement," Beast said in that monotone that was now not so benign.

Aurora swayed where she sat, but Beetle steadied her.

"Lilith's vessel gave birth to the baby?" I asked.

"Yes," Beast replied, "but it was unsuccessful. The baby was too small, so they discarded it. This was their first successful incubation, but the child was born too small."

Aurora's face was wet, and tears dripped onto her shirt. Her eyes were fixed on something far distant, maybe the date tree, but I thought it was even farther away.

"There have been others?" I asked.

"The bosses had not been able to successfully incubate an offspring before," said Beast. "They have investigated, but their conclusions were less than optimal."

The Returned were just like us. They couldn't have kids. That part made sense. What confused me was that they weren't using their own bodies; they were using the bodies of their vessels.

"It's not the bodies," Aurora said without moving. "If that's what you're thinking. The knights don't possess other hosts, but you occupy flesh that is not really yours. The flesh isn't the problem. It's probably the magic."

Beast nodded. "The incubation was successful because it incorporated some cog magic, too, magic the bosses took from Ace."

Aurora looked at me and huffed.

"You have Ace's body, and Ace's magic helped to make me, so you're my father *again*," she said looking at me.

"Can't seem to avoid it," I said, and wished with all my heart that I could give her the kind of loving look that would have helped her, a little, anyway.

The little shade offered by the outcropping shrunk on one side and grew on the other as the twin suns overhead moved through the sky. Even with two stars, the light and heat were tepid things.

"Who was in the vessel that contributed the sperm?" Aurora asked, without facing Beast.

"Satariel," Beast responded. "Post-birth," he paused, "Post-your-birth," he corrected, "Lilith and Satariel left their vessels and returned. The Corner Office did Victory Lap, but I knew the truth. Ace helped me to fabricate my death, so that I could explore anti-boss options."

"And I killed him," I said, as quietly as a cog could speak.

"You have taken much from me," Beast agreed, "including my head in your world."

"Correction," said Ant, "the other side of our world, B-E7-10."

"Excellent effort," replied Beast, "But I am not mistaken. These two come from another world entirely. Somewhere beyond the suns. It is the place where the bosses began, and they are a race that will forever subjugate and torment us. It is their nature."

I wanted to disagree, to tell him that we were not the oppressors, that the bosses, the Returned, were the only enemies, but my arguments would have rung hollow. I had killed his lover. My fellow human beings were the architects of all of the suffering in his world, and they were trying to do the same to mine.

"We are not the same, he and I," Aurora said, blinking, as if from a dream and pointing toward me.

"No," said Beast. "You can touch our network."

"And your power can flow through me," Aurora added.

"She has maximum optimization," said Ant. He and Beetle lowered their heads.

"That's how you were able to bring the wind," I guessed.

Aurora nodded.

"I can do very little without their help, but when I am in touch with the network, I can harness all of their emotional energy, their frustration and love and hatred and joy. It would be more than I could handle if I tried to take it all in. I suppose the Returned, the bosses, can't access the network."

"They have tried, but their power in the network is so weak, we just ignore them. They are not connected to us and not strong enough to force their way in. They know about our connection, though, and they will stop at nothing to keep up from joining together. They have hundreds of cunning ways to keep us from joining," said Beast.

"Incentives," said Zephyr, "for turning in other cogs who make contact."

"Promotions for those who inform on the leaders outside of the company," added Beetle.

"It is deeper than that," said Beast. "They teach us, from the moment of decantation that we must compete with all the others. We can only be happy if we vanquish all of the other cogs and rise in The Company. 'The cream rises to the top,' they say."

"This is a question opportunity I wanted to outreach to you," said Ant. "Is cream a flying machine, or some kind of inflatable? How does it rise?"

In a world without mothers, without the nurture of breasts and milk, how could we explain?

"It is a saying from our world that doesn't matter here, except to keep you from uniting against them. If they keep you fighting each other, you will never realize that you could take over, make this world your own," said Aurora. "There are those who do the same thing in our world, and it has the same effect."

"You did not kill Ace," Beast said, not looking at me. "It was his choice. We knew of this baby that was a part of us." He raised his arms to his side and slapped them down forcefully. "We worried that the bosses would corrupt her, so we made a playbook. Ace gave his life to bring you here so that you could bring Aurora to us. He died so that she could free us from the bosses."

"And our success metrics would have been high indeed if it wasn't for that traitor, Z-4HW0," Beetle said, and he farted.

Ant and Beast farted in return.

"Perhaps you, too, could have a network to oppose the bosses?" Ant asked.

"We could if we were brave enough, but we don't, because we aren't"

"I have never heard it put so succinctly before," I said, hoping that she could see the pride on my expressionless face. She was not pleased though, and I thought she looked at me differently than she had just a few moments before.

Aurora stood and dusted herself off.

"I think I can open the window to our world with your help, B-E7-10, but I'm not going to do it until we figure out how to give you what I've got."

"The magic?" Beast asked.

"The magic," Aurora answered.

"We're almost out of time," I interjected.

"You took his love and his joy, even if the life was freely given. You'll have to wait until we're finished," Aurora said, and strode off toward the mountain, the other cogs shuffling behind.

Twenty

We ascended through scrub up a dirt path between the boulders. The dirt had been disturbed, and there were tracks I didn't recognize, but not, by the look of them, the prints of cog shoes. Beast led the way, stopping only occasionally to listen or look at the sky.

While he was staring upward, two animals dashed past us across the hillside. The sudden movement startled Beast, toppling him backwards into Beetle, who knocked down Ant, who stopped when Aurora caught him.

"What was that?" she asked.

"Wulee," the cogs said together.

"They are meat," said Beetle.

"And protected by law," added Ant.

"Only licensed harvesters have the opportunity to harm them," Beast explained. "They are the meat for our stew. We let them roam in the wild so that we do not have the mess and smell of domesticating them."

"And they breed so quickly," said Ant, "That they are abundant, species-wise."

The wulee looked like a cross between a kangaroo and a rabbit. It had short arms and ran on its larger back legs. It's ears were very long and hung down around its flat face.

"Are they dangerous?" I asked.

Cog grunt-laughing was my response. So I'm new in town, sheesh.

"They consume plants," Beast said, "and are consumed by many other animals. The violence is not bi-directional, though. They are impressive in the speed arena, and they leverage their iterative reproduction to maximize success parameters. Those two are in a mating race. The female races with available males. When the female wins, she chooses her mate among the losers."

Aurora snorted.

"Sounds like a good system to me," she said. "Do the males ever win?"

"No," said Beast. "That is one reason why we eat them."

"The female piece is suboptimal for us," Ant advised.

Aurora raised an eyebrow.

"Oh?"

"Not you," Beast corrected. "In your world there are many females. My observation is that they are not as efficient and forward moving as males in your world. They do not have maximal velocity or power. The bosses said that is why we don't decant any females. They say females make life difficult."

"What does Lilith think of that?" I asked.

They rocked from foot to foot.

"Lilith expresses frustration in the basement of the SWE," said Beetle.

I was familiar with how Lilith expressed her frustration, and I was familiar with that basement.

"You are not like Lilith," said Beast to Aurora. "And the bosses are wrong about the females of your world. They have all been defeated by one of the knights who is a woman, and they fear her, even if they won't say it."

"Her name is Augustine," I said. "She is our general."

Aurora stared along the path where the wulees had disappeared.

"How do they reproduce? The wulees, I mean," she asked.

"They mate-partner, then the female lays eggs," explained Beast.

"Usually six eggs," said Ant.

"How soon after the race do they mate-partner?"

Beast considered.

"Very soon after," he said at last. "The latency is small."

"Could those that ran past have done it already, the mate partnering?" Aurora asked.

"Perhaps," Beast replied.

"When does she lay the eggs?"

"She will lay them when the suns go down," Beast said.

"Then we've only got a little time," Aurora declared, trotting after the wulees.

We shambled behind her through a long hallway of rock until we emerged on a semicircular flat ledge. There was a cave mouth at one end and a sheer drop at the other. Just inside the cave we could see movement. Then sand sprayed out of the entrance as if a badger were digging into a hillside.

"They are constructing a nest for the eggs," said Beast.

"Listen," Aurora said, taking Beast by the shoulders. "I think the way the bosses made me had something to do with beginning life, a spirit completely empty, a clean slate to write on. They gave me power from the Ether and from our own world."

"What is the Ether?" Ant asked.

"This," said Beast, his arms taking in the scene. "Where we live. They call it the Ether."

"I think I can give magic to a new life as well. I think I can leave my power, the power that comes from you, from the Ether, in something that isn't a cog, something the bosses didn't mass produce. I think I should invest my power from the Ether in one of these animals."

"But they are just beasts," Beetle said. "They will not be operational the way we are."

"Maybe they could be," Aurora said. "I want to leave all the power I have from this realm in this realm. It really belongs to you. It comes from you, and the bosses stole it. But the bosses made you unable to wield this power outside of the network, so I have to put it somewhere it can be wielded. I have to invest something that can join your network, allow your power to flow through it, like it flows through me."

"The animal will need to be guided," Beast said. "And it will need a male progenitor, just as Satariel was yours."

I gritted my teeth at that reminder, but my anger wasn't of any use to me here and now. I swallowed it down. I still didn't grok Aurora's plan.

"Beast," Aurora began, "I can put your consciousness into the male wulee. He has already given his seed, but you will be able to connect with the offspring."

"What will become of my body while I am inside the wulee?"

"Your friends will have to watch over it as the knights are watching over my father back in our world. When you leave the wulee, it will die, but you can protect and teach the young. You can help them to think and to make use of their new gifts."

"We will care for your body," said Ant. "Will he be able to speak to us?"

"I don't have any idea," Aurora replied. "But he should still be able to connect with you." She pointed to her head.

Beast held his right arm out straight and grasped the shoulders of the others one-by-one. When he came to me, he put his arm down.

"I have so many feelings about you, knight. You are a killer, but you brought us Aurora. I hope that we may meet again, in this world or in yours, and that when we do, we will not fight."

"We will eat pizza," I said, and was reminded again that cogs don't have tears to shed.

Beast nodded and turned toward Aurora.

"The suns are low. We should make haste."

Twenty-One

Aurora knelt in the middle of the ledge. The digging from inside the cave stopped. She whispered, and the two wulee emerged, whiskers twitching. They took tentative steps toward her, then retreated. She kept absolutely still, and Beast beside her did the same. All the while Aurora whispered, and the animals eventually drew close. When they were about a meter from her, they sat, then lay down on the warm stone and went still.

"Are you ready B-07-10?"

"I am ready Aurora, knight of the Order of St. John."

He reached his hand to her and when it touched her hip, her body lit with a light I had never seen before in this world or in our own. It was a rich golden light, so dense with color that it looked as if her body were actually coated with the precious metal. The light expanded, encompassing Beast and the two wulees. Beast's body became like a pile of rags, collapsing to the ground. The surrounding light retreated to Aurora, and she became a golden statue, her arm extended, unmoving, unbreathing. Beneath her, the wulee stirred.

The male stood first. He extended his fingers while he looked at each digit. He twitched his ears and squinted his eyes before stretching each leg. The female wulee rose, shaking her head as if to shoo an insect. Her body was taller than the male, and the short hair on her chest and belly was lighter than the rest. She ambled into the cave, and the male followed her.

Beetle and Ant took my hands and hummed, and I was inside the cave, looking through the male's eyes.

"This is a fine body," said a voice in my head. "The senses are sharp and varied, and it moves with speed." The voice was filled with awe, the tones and cadence varied.

"Is that you Beast?" asked Ant.

"It is me," the voice said. "I am remade. Tell me, Aurora, how will I ever return to my body? When I left your world, it was as if I had been blinded. I mourned for months the loss of your senses, the emotions running through your body. Now I feel again the wind on my skin, the smell of urine in the cave, the sound of my own voice."

Aurora didn't answer, but as the male turned toward the female, she was illuminated by a faint glowing from behind her. She stepped aside to reveal a clutch of pale green eggs, which looked incongruous in the grey of the cave. They were lit from within, throwing the female's shadow across the wall. The male crossed to her, and they touched ears, remaining still until the cave was in full darkness.

The female lifted her head, hearing something, and the male reached out a paw. She rubbed her furry cheek against his, then collapsed like a puppet whose strings have been cut. The male pushed at her, lifting her arms to let them fall, stroking her ears.

Beetle and Ant broke the connection, and I was standing in the dark, hidden by the rocks at the side of the flat ledge. The gold of Aurora's statue slid off her as if melting and slithered like quicksilver into the cave.

Then Beast screamed. The wulee he occupied made a sound like the wailing of banshees. It was amplified by the cave and echoed off the hillsides around us. It was a sound of such profound grief and loss that it felt as if my heart was being physically pulled from my chest. I was consumed with visions of lovers and friends, of families that had raised me, and of all the knights' incarnations. They were all gone, all dead, and the weight of their passing landed on me with the force of a mountain. If I live another thousand years, I will live with the agony of that scream every day.

Aurora fell to her knees and sobbed, finally putting her face in her hands, her shoulders heaving. We stood still, dealing with the pain of that scream for a long time. Perhaps it was just a moment and only felt like hours. Time moves differently in the Ether.

Eventually I staggered forward and touched Aurora.

"We should get Beast's body back to the city," I said. "They will need to get him set up, a system to feed him and give him water."

"There is no need," Ant said. "Beast has made his choice."

"What do you mean?" I asked and moved toward Beast's body. "What choice?"

"He's gone, dad," Aurora said and sighed. "He and the eggs have my magic now, and he doesn't want the body the bosses made for him."

"I will use *this* body," said a slurring voice in the darkness. The male wulee strode out of the cave. "Getting used to the mouth," he said.

"Beast?" I asked.

"Now you call me Faare," he said. The voice was awkward, but full of inflection. "These animals," he stopped, "the wulee, have some awareness, and they have a simple language. Faare means messenger, 'one who brings.' I will be the messenger now."

The cogs all spoke at the same time, but Faare silenced them with a look.

"This is no way to repay Aurora's great gift," Faare said, and we were around the date palm in the blink of an eye.

"You can teleport?" I asked, rocking back and forth from foot to foot.

Faare winked at me, and I recognized it immediately as the wink I had seen on the severed head of the senior director back in New Hampshire before he was sucked into the whirlwind.

Above us the leaves of the date palm rustled impatiently, the crown now drooping with fruit.

"I'm sorry I can't be here to help you raise the children," Aurora said, looking at Faare with a wistful smile.

"You have love waiting for you," Faare said. "I saw her in your mind. Go to her, free your world as I and our, uh, *children*, will free this one. He touched his chest, and a faint glow appeared. On seeing it, the other cogs joined hands, finally clasping his furry paws. The glow spread into a sphere that rose from their little circle. It grew until it was as big as the palm tree.

It split in the middle and the crack pulled open to reveal the deck of a ship. Augustine and Peter were bent over Paul's body. Peter was doing chest compressions while Augustine drew something from a vial into a syringe. The sun was hard and bright behind them. Augustine looked haggard, and I could tell Peter was praying under his breath.

Aurora looked at each of the cogs in turn, then touched her own chest where a faint glow sputtered and disappeared. She grabbed me by the arm and leapt through the rip in dimensions.

Twenty-Two

I sat up gasping, knocking Peter off his feet, and saw Aurora roll onto the deck. Little purple footballs fell beside her as she landed, and then a torrent of the things rushed out of the Ether, so many that the boat listed with their weight before the rift closed.

Water lapped against the boat, a gust of wind whooshed by, making my sweaty scalp cool. Aurora staggered to her feet, brushing dates off of her pants. The little footballs were ripe dates, perhaps a ton of them, their purple skins reflecting the harsh sunlight.

No one spoke. I was still catching my breath. Aurora looked dazed from the fall. Peter and Augustine stared at me, then Aurora, then the dates. The spell was broken when Barbara appeared.

"It's about time," she grumbled. "I kept that window open for four hours, four hours! I was so exhausted I had to lie down, and half an hour later here you are. You didn't need my help after all."

My joints were stiff and painful, and I had lost some weight. My throat was horribly dry, so I motioned for some water. Augustine realized she was still holding the syringe. She capped the needle and deposited it in a sharps container next to my bed.

She poured a glass of water and set it down beside me. When she reached toward my face, I pulled away, forgetting that I still had a feeding tube in. She stripped the tape from my nose and in one smooth movement, pulled the tube out all the way from my stomach. I coughed a little as the tip passed my vocal chords but was otherwise unhurt.

The water burned at first, and I sputtered but kept drinking. When I was on my third glass I thought about peeing and realized there was still another tube to be removed. Before I could ask for the supplies to pull out my urinary catheter, there was a little pop from the end of the boat with the big pile of dates.

Aurora took a step back as two more of the dates popped, then like popcorn in a pan, they all started popping. With each pop a little cloud of bugs flew up into the air.

"What the fuck?" Augustine said.

"No clue," I replied.

As the little bugs rose from the boat, they swirled in a cloud above us. The cloud grew darker and bigger until, as if at a signal we couldn't hear, the bugs dispersed in every direction. They left a sticky, slippery mess behind them.

Peter crept toward the pile of empty date skins and retrieved one that still had a tiny wriggling bug in it. He closed his fingers around the date, trapping the bug inside and strode away into the cabin.

"That was weird," Aurora said, arriving beside Augustine, who threw her arms around Aurora's neck and squeezed her.

I guessed Augustine was crying because Aurora patted her head and made soft, reassuring noises. Finally, Augustine pushed herself away from her and took a deep breath.

"I'm so glad you made it home safely," Augustine said cordially.

"You missed me, then?" Aurora asked, a crooked smile spreading slowly across her face.

"I missed you a great deal," Augustine replied, and while her eyes glistened, no tears fell. "We have so much work to do."

They both looked at me disapprovingly.

"Can I take my catheter out first? Is that too much to ask?"

We convened in the large central room in the yacht's cabin after a shower and a shave and a meal. It was only a sandwich, but after three days of little to nothing to eat, and that only gruel and stew, it tasted as if Gordon Ramsey himself, had spread the mustard and sliced the cheese. While I was shaving, I made faces, stretching the muscles in my face to reassure myself that I could.

Thomas, Peter, Augustine, Aurora, and I were the only knights present. The other six were back in the US of A, thwarting Garridan Roosevelt, aka Thaumiel. As we were on a wartime footing, Augustine chaired the meeting. Peter may be our chairman, but his talents run to politics and human resources; Augustine is our general.

"Where's Simon?" Aurora asked.

"Mission," Thomas replied.

"Let's get a report from the Ether before I bring you up to speed on what's going on here," Augustine said, and typed something on her laptop.

I tilted my chin towards Aurora, who cleared her throat.

"Right," she began, "the Ether. First, it turns out I am the scion of an unholy alliance between Satariel and Lilith. They used hosts to successfully conceive a child, me, but they thought the child was too small to live, so they threw it in a dumpster."

That's my girl. She doesn't bury the lead. A cloud passed over Augustine's face, but she said nothing.

"Secondly, it turns out there is magic in the Ether, it's just not available to you guys, the knights, I mean."

"*She*, however, wielded it quite effectively," I interjected.

"We hypothesize it is because that some cog magic was used in my conception. The magic was taken from the very cog that Dad, uh, Paul possessed. We're not exactly sure, but that's all in the past now. I divested myself of my Ether magic. I don't yet know how it will effect my power here."

"Divested how?" Thomas said, leaning forward. "How do you just give up your magic?"

"She gave it to a sentient kangaroo," I said, which brought such a withering glare from Aurora that I censored myself. "That was ignorant and childish. Aurora helped to bring about a new species of sentient being in the Ether who will likely be an ally if not a friend. Aurora is the cause for their alliance, and I, I'm afraid, am the reason we won't be friends."

"I can give you the details later," Aurora said. "I want Augustine to know that now the Returned will be fighting on two fronts, here and at home. Their heavy hitters, Thaumiel and Lilith are here, so the wulee might have a chance against the Returned's rear guard."

122

"The woolie?" Peter asked.

"Wulee," Aurora replied. "WOO-lee."

Peter made a note in his notebook, and Thomas raised an eyebrow.

"Is that the species or the individual?" he asked.

"Wulee is the species," said Aurora. "The individual is called Faare, the messenger."

Twenty-Three

"That's a lot to unpack," said Augustine. Aurora and I visibly winced. When Augustine tilted her head questioningly, I groaned and Aurora chuckled.

"Cogspeak," I explained.

"Ah," said Augustine. "Moving forward, I,"

Our laughter interrupted her. The others in the room eyed us suspiciously.

"Cogspeak, again," I said.

"Okay," Augustine began, "if the two of you are done playing, let's talk about operations on the mainland."

Aurora and I dared not look at each other. Besides, Augustine's tone said unequivocally that she would brook no further interruption.

"We knew that Roosevelt was organizing 're-education' camps in each of the eleven federal districts. So far, to avoid charges of racism from the dwindling number of democratic nations, he has only been sending left-wing activists and intellectuals, about twenty thousand have been detained so far, that we know of. It almost goes without saying that he has closed the borders. What surprised us is that he has closed them both ways; nobody's getting out either. Coyotes are now smuggling people *into* Mexico," Augustine said.

"I'm guessing it's not just farm workers heading home," I said.

"There are some," she replied, "but also lots of terrified white people. They're driving the cost of crossing the border so high that soon the farm workers won't be able to afford it. On the northern border a group of Canadian pirates who call themselves 'Bruins' is smuggling people to the maritime provinces in boats."

"These are the things we can confirm," Peter explained. "These and the food rationing and the mandatory prayers in schools."

"Don't forget loyalty oaths," Thomas spat.

"The Supreme Court outlawed those decades ago," Aurora said, raising her voice.

"Overturned just last week," replied Thomas.

"His master stroke is the amendment amendment," said Augustine. "He is trying to amend Article V of the constitution to make other amendments easier. He can extend his term of office, create a state religion, or anything else he wants without having to go to all the states for approval."

"No one is opposing him?" Aurora asked, incredulous.

"We're opposing him," said Thomas with a bitter smile.

"There are groups," Augustine confirmed, "but remember those re-education camps? The government is monitoring internet and cell phone communications. They've got plenty of tech, but I'd bet that Ghagiel is infusing their algorithms with magic. Chaos in a rule-bound system, that's his bread and butter."

"He is single-handedly responsible for the modern French bureaucracy," said Peter.

"In short," Augustine said, picking up the narrative, "the resistance is fractured, harassed, and out-gunned, literally and figuratively. Due to a series of impossible coincidences, three supreme court justices died before Roosevelt even took office, and the Senate filibustered any new appointments. He replaced the justices with lackeys, and they're going to give him everything he wants: unrestricted constitutional right to concealed weapon carry, overturning *Roe v. Wade*, gutting the Environmental Protection Agency, and the loyalty oath case that Thomas mentioned. The loyalty oath case was expedited, and the others are due for decision in the Spring term. There was a case to prohibit prayer in schools, but it was withdrawn. The litigants saw the writing on the wall."

"Hold it," I said. "The election was just three months ago."

"You were gone longer than three days, Paul," said Barbara.

Now I looked at my compatriots in earnest for the first time since returning. They were noticeably older than when I had left.

I hung my head.

"How long?"

"Four months," said Thomas.

"The cost?"

"Ten years for the three of us. Barbara opened the window to the Ether every day as long as she could. She didn't age, but-"

"It took a toll," Barbara said coolly.

Peter looked at his watch.

"The refreshments are late," he complained, rising and exiting toward the kitchen. He swore loudly in Italian a minute later, and we rushed to him. The cook and the steward were on the floor, necks and faces bloated, eyes swimming in swollen cheeks. Peter was on his knees checking the steward's pulse, but we had all seen enough corpses to know these two were long gone.

Augustine and I knelt by the cook, checking his body for signs of trauma.

"This looks like anaphylaxis, like a massive immune system reaction," Augustine said.

"Did they eat something?" I asked.

"The food is still on the counter," Aurora replied. "I can't tell if anything is missing or not."

"Got something," said Thomas, holding up the steward's arm.

Everyone but Peter leaned in to look at it. Peter continued a constant stream of curses under his breath while shaking his head.

"Looks like a bug bite," offered Augustine. "Maybe a mosquito."

"We're more than a hundred miles from shore," replied Thomas. "How the hell is a mosquito going to get out here?"

"Maybe there's a small population on the boat?" I guessed.

Thomas pursed his lips, obviously tamping down an angry response.

"Oh fuck," Aurora murmured, and the penny dropped.

"The bugs from the Ether."

Twenty-Four

Thomas and Peter bent over a magnifying glass studying the last Ether bug we had aboard, the one Peter had kept. It was dead, but the two men used tweezers and a pocketknife to see what they could see. It looked like any old mosquito to me, but I don't know anything about creepy-crawlies, so I kept quiet and awaited their verdict.

Peter pointed at the bug's abdomen with the tip of his knife.

"See how the abdomen is swollen," he said.

"That's what they look like when they've drunk your blood. When I was a kid, I used to pop them," I said helpfully.

"Charming," Peter replied. "I captured this specimen while it was emerging from one of the dates. It couldn't possibly have bitten anyone."

"Maybe it drank juice from the date."

"I think that's right," said Thomas. "But these are not ordinary dates. I enchanted them to grow without considering they would ever return to this world. They are made of the soil and water and nutrients from the Ether."

"They are not of this world," I said in a melodramatic voice.

"Please, Paul," Peter chastised. "We think this is what killed our steward and the cook. When they were bitten, some of the date substance must have been injected in their bodies."

"Couldn't have been very much," I murmured.

"Precisely," Peter replied. "It only took that tiny amount to kill them."

"Should we be wearing full hazmat suits?" I asked. "What if they bite us?"

"I have been bitten," said Thomas, showing me a welt on his shoulder. "Nothing happened."

"I have posited that it is because the Ether is not new to us. We have been exposed many times," Peter explained.

"Not in these bodies," I argued.

"Aurora has told me more about your trip in the Ether. She believes that in some ways, our physical bodies are irrelevant, that we carry memories and energies that affect our biology. She thinks it is why we cannot have children. We are too old, and when we died, all of our procreative power died with us. It makes her birth all the more remarkable. I think we carry magical antibodies that protects us against substances from the Ether, as it no doubt protects the Returned."

"Not anyone else, though," said Thomas.

"Except Roosevelt and the other Returned in this world," I said, repeating Peter.

"If we're right, yeah," Thomas replied.

"You didn't think a mosquito could make it to this boat from shore," I said. "So those bugs shouldn't be able to get there either, right?"

"I guess we'll find out," said Thomas.

Aurora was shoveling date skins off the deck when I found her.

"How you feeling?" I asked.

She grunted, which brought me back to those years when that was the only response I could get from her.

"I was thrown away," she said, heaving a shovelful of dates over the side.

"Those may be toxic," I said. We should probably bag and secure them.

She nodded.

"I'm devil-spawn."

I took her shoulders and craned my neck to look into her downturned face.

"You are Aurora St. Paul, Knight of the Order of St. John. You are my beloved daughter, beloved sister to all the knights. It was not your choice how you came into the world; you didn't have anything to do with it. But I am so glad you did come. Besides, if some part of you comes from the Returned, then I might hate them a little less."

"You're such a dork," she said, but she smiled a sad smile and put down the shovel. "Part of me is still back in the Ether."

"I know, and part of you will never forgive me for taking over Ace's body. I will have to live with that." I thought of the scream of heartbreak from Beast, Faare, I mean, and I was laden with the guilt of Ace's death all over again.

"I know you wouldn't have done it if there was another way," she admitted. "And I understand that they used you to get to me. I know you have killed many people over the centuries, and that some of those killings may not have been just. Still, I didn't know any of the people you killed or their families."

I know she added the last part to make it more accurate, not to hurt me, but 'their families' drove home how much damage I had caused the other cogs.

We were quiet for a while in the stillness before the sun disappeared over the horizon.

"Remember how it freaked me out that you had illuminated those manuscripts in the fourteen hundreds, that book you gave me for Christmas one year?" she asked.

"I remember."

"It was the same thing then," she said. "I knew you had been a monk, a brother, or whatever, all those centuries ago, but seeing your paintings, *your paintings*,"

"Illuminations," I corrected, but she ignored me.

"It was evidence that you were really there, that you were really nine hundred years old. I thought I knew, but I didn't really know."

"And you didn't really *know* that I was a killer until the Ether," I said so softly I wondered if she heard me.

"It's stupid, I know," she said, frowning. "*I'm* a killer. Hell, you watched me do it."

"But you didn't know him or his family. It was just a righteous act of war."

"Yeah," she said. She put her hands on the small of her back and leaned backward until she heard a satisfying crack. "Guess I better get some biohazard bags."

I touched her arm to stop her.

"I love you, Aurora. I always will."

"I know," she said, her lovely face so tired and troubled. "I love you, too."

Twenty-Five

Simon's eyes kept drooping while he was giving his report. He had only had a couple of hours of sleep in three days. The room behind him was recognizable to anyone who has ever slept in the call room at a hospital: bunk beds, a round table, a counter with a coffee maker and a toaster. He spoke to us via a relay that James had MacGyvered using our satellite phones. The bunks behind him were empty, and he looked over his shoulder at them longingly before continuing.

"It is, as you guys have seen, massive histamine reactions and almost instant hypoxia, like the entire immune system attacks its host. The CDC says it isn't a virus, but an 'unknown toxin.' They have figured out it has a vector, but they think it's ordinary mosquitoes," said Simon, yawning.

"Protocols to prevent infection should be the same as with Malaria, then," said Peter.

"The problem is that the Ether mosquitoes bite during the day as well as at night. They don't stay in wet or shady areas. They're everywhere." Simon pushed his hair back from his forehead. "They've got bug zappers in the hallways of the hospital. If there weren't a shortage, they'd have them in every room."

"WHO is reporting a mortality rate of over eighty percent," said Thomas from outside the frame on the computer.

"Fewer people are dying in developing countries," Simon replied. "There are fewer autoimmune diseases in the developing world. Lots of theories why that is, but not much research. We're not overrun on the floors or in the ICU, because the patients usually die in the ED."

"No treatments at all?" I asked, incredulous.

"Sometimes the IV cetirizine helps, but they have to administer it in time. There's like, no incubation period for this. A few minutes after they get bitten, their throat closes, and they suffocate." Simon paused. "The bodies are stacking up so badly that administration is starting to worry about secondary epidemics like meningitis and cholera."

Simon's eyes closed for a moment and his head rocked forward, jarring him awake.

"And the health care workers?" Peter asked.

"The ones who stay in full PPE, the moon suits, are safe from the bugs while they're here. We've lost about a third of the staff once they go home," said Simon and yawned again.

"Get some rest," Peter said, and broke the connection.

"Some of the world media is down," I said. "There are networks without enough people left to keep broadcasting."

"Speak of the devil," Augustine said, spinning her laptop to face us. CNN was broadcasting from the White House press room. The podium was empty, but a tall acrylic tube was stationed beside it. The camera closed in on the tube, which showed that it was swarming with Ether mosquitoes.

"What the fuck," Aurora murmured.

Garridan Roosevelt strode to the podium, a man on a mission. The camera panned to the gallery where reporters usually sat, but there were only four people there in full-body Tyvek suits, cameras on their shoulders. Roosevelt adjusted the microphone.

"The mainstream media would have you believe that we are in a crisis," he said. "But as usual, my people are rejecting the hysteria and fear-mongering that the big networks will use to drive up their ratings. The love drama, don't they?" Here he chuckled to himself.

"I'm here to tell you all that this is nonsense. It is a hoax of the most vicious variety. You do not have to wear suits like these idiots here." The camera panned to the four cameramen in Tyvek. "This is what the liberal and the progressives, whatever they are calling themselves these days want you to think. 'Be afraid,' they shout. 'The end is nigh' or some such nonsense. This is a communist plot to take over, simple as that. It is a conspiracy to deny the American people the benefits of their votes, the benefits of their properly elected government. And I'm gonna prove it to you right now."

In the background was a thump. The camera moved towards the sound to show a Secret Service agent on the ground, clutching his throat, his heels drumming on the floor, face growing lobster red while it swelled. The screen went black for a moment and was replaced by the shield of Homeland Security. Then the picture returned, showing Roosevelt taking off his jacket and rolling up one sleeve. He stepped to the cylinder where we could now make out a rubber gasket at the height of his shoulder.

Roosevelt pushed his arm through the gasket, and it was immediately swarmed by mosquitoes. He turned to the camera and gave a slow smile, a Thaumiel smile, as if he was looking at us through the camera. A timer appeared in the upper right corner of the screen. When it reached one minute, he shook his arm inside the cylinder and carefully slid it out.

"Let's get a close-up," he said genially, and the camera zoomed in to show that his arm was spotted with bites. A man in a lab coat appeared next to the president and listened to his chest with a stethoscope. He took the president's pulse while Roosevelt stared at us through the camera. The man in the lab coat smiled, eyebrows raised, and gave the camera an enthusiastic thumbs up.

As the camera moved back to Roosevelt's face, the man in the lab coat slid away behind him, but the microphone could not hide the gasping, choking sounds, no matter how much the president raised his voice.

"Do we surrender?" Aurora asked.

"The Returned are like Klingons," Thomas replied. "They don't take prisoners."

Dear Readers,

Thanks for spending some time with me and the Council of the Order of St. John. As you can probably guess, this isn't the end of the adventure for the K-Nurses. The amazing Phil Thron narrated the audiobook for *The Road to Damascus,* which takes the story to a whole new level.

I truly appreciate you taking the time to read my work, even if it wasn't for you. In that vein, I'd like to ask a favor. Whatever you thought of the book, good or bad, I will be in your debt if you could leave a review on Amazon.com or Goodreads.com.

Every review helps to establish the book's place in the literary world and makes it possible to keep the series going.

I hope it gives the general public some insight into the tremendous challenges nurses face today. Everyone says nurses are heroes, but that sentiment has become hollow and a poor excuse for the kind of support nurses really need. They give of themselves even when they are discouraged and burned out. If this book gives you a little peek into their world, so much the better.

Thanks for reading and all my best wishes,

Mark Leo Tapper

Other K-Nurse books available from Amazon.com:

The Road to Damascus: K-Nurse 1
The Left Hand of God: K-Nurse 1.5
But a Wandering Voice: K-Nurse 2
The Singer of Thrace :   K-Nurse 3
Between the Dragon and His Wrath: K-Nurse 4
In the Wilds and Mountains I Hunt: K-Nurse 5
In Thy Absence   K-Nurse 6

Mark Leo Tapper is the Award-Winning author of *The Vials of Our Wrath*. He lives, works as a nurse, and writes speculative fiction from the home he shares with his wife Susannah, stepsons Arthur and Felix, and several STET pets, in Vermont.

You can find out more about the author and his books at MarkLeoTapper.com. Sign up at the website to receive news of events, new K-Nurse releases, and download deals.

The audiobook of **The Road to Damascus**, narrated by Phil Thron, is available from Audible.com

www.ingramcontent.com/pod-product-compliance
Lightning Source LLC
Chambersburg PA
CBHW050737230626
47052CB00002BA/467